VEGAS DOC'S ACCIDENTAL "I DO"

RACHEL DOVE

Recycling programs for this product may not exist in your area

ISBN-13: 978-1-335-95290-5

Vegas Doc's Accidental "I Do"

For questions and comments about the quality of this book, please contact us at CustomerService@Harlequin.com.

Harlequin Enterprises ULC
22 Adelaide St. West, 41st Floor
Toronto, Ontario M5H 4E3, Canada
www.Harlequin.com

HarperCollins Publishers
Macken House, 39/40 Mayor Street Upper
Dublin 1, D01 C9W8, Ireland
www.HarperCollins.com

Printed in U.S.A.

1 2 3 4 5 6 7 8 9 10 HDC 29 28 27 26

Flashes of the night before came screaming back at her as she scanned the unfamiliar hotel room surroundings.

Her, drinking with the other interns on the Strip. Sebastian, coming along with his teasing and his dares. The pair of them, having some kind of dance-off to Taylor Swift while a crowd cheered them on. Sebastian, daring her to drink that Day-Glo shot that looked like fluorescent snot and didn't taste much better. Sebastian, tipping her back and kissing her hard—

Oh god. *What the heck was that? Delete.* That didn't happen, right? She could never be drunk enough to snog Brown. There wasn't enough alcohol in Vegas to make that image a possibility. She blinked hard, as though she could reboot her gray matter. More images came loose, and she reached for them with trepidation.

Sebastian, laughing as an Elvis impersonator read from a book. The same Elvis telling them to smile as he took a photo of them both, Seb's arms wrapped tight around her as they said a very inebriated version of cheese to the camera. Seb's hand in hers as she pushed a circle of gold over his thick knuckle.

Dear Reader,

Thanks for reading yet another medical roller coaster! I appreciate each and every one of you and love to hear from readers. Taylor and Seb were so much fun to write, I could feel the tension between them from the start—and I knew it was going to be a wild time in Vegas!

Looking forward to bringing you more high-tension medical romances in the coming months—till then, thank you for your love and support.

Happy reading!

Rachel Dove

Rachel Dove is a writer and teacher living in West Yorkshire with her husband, their two sons and their animals. In July 2015, she won the *Prima* magazine and Mills & Boon Flirty Fiction Competition. She was the winner of the Writers Bureau Writer of the Year Award in 2016. She has had work published in the UK and overseas in various magazines and newspaper publications.

Books by Rachel Dove

Harlequin Medical Romance

Fighting for the Trauma Doc's Heart
The Paramedic's Secret Son
Falling for the Village Vet
Single Mom's Mistletoe Kiss
A Midwife, Her Best Friend, Their Family
How to Resist Your Rival
A Baby to Change Their Lives
Faking It with the Firefighter
One Night to Twin Surprise
Hating Dr. Sunshine

Visit the Author Profile page at Harlequin.com.

This one's for you, Pops!

Ditto

Love from Lemon Legs

CHAPTER ONE

"MOM, I CARRIED out a successful running whip stitch on a beating heart last night. I think I can manage to do a load of laundry. Being raised by you two, how could I not?" Taylor said as she closed her locker with a flourish and winked impishly at Selina, who laughed and stuck her nose back in her book on obstetrics. That was Selina, ever thirsty for knowledge on her speciality. Whenever she wasn't working, she was researching, reading other people's articles, suggesting new strategies to her department that might make a difference. She came across as a girlie girl, but underneath she was just like Taylor. Driven and determined to be the best. Tired, too. Taylor had almost forgotten that one. They were both killing it at work, but the thought of getting a break at the end of this was looking more welcoming by the minute.

The coed locker room was relatively quiet, given that the pair of them had come in early for rounds. Or, truth be told, they'd both stayed late the night before and decided to crash in one of the empty patient rooms till the sun broke through the clouds and woke them both from their power nap. Well, the early bird got the worm, right? At least that's what Taylor's grandmother had always taught her. Taylor could hear her now in the background of her phone call, muttering something to her mother. The two Cousins women who had raised her *always* got the worm. And would probably use them as bait to catch bigger birds.

"Taylor, your grandmother wants to know whether you are wearing the kidney warmers today, because she knows for a fact that you are no doubt down to the big, ugly pants."

The tone of her mother's voice was firm, but she could hear the suppressed laughter and warmth under the words. *Busted.* She really needed to stop telling her family every boring detail of her life. Which apparently, outside the realm of her work, which she couldn't really talk about, amounted to big underwear and her lack of time for chores.

"She also wants me to point out that lying to your elders is decidedly frowned upon, even for a big-shot doctor."

"Fine," Taylor laughed, pulling the waistband of her scrub trousers down and seeing the telltale thick band of what were, to be fair, pretty ugly and decidedly unsexy underwear that her grandmother labeled kidney warmers, because, well…they were big and pretty much covered her up better than a chastity belt ever could. Which was also laughable since she never had time to date, let alone flash her underwear at a member of the opposite sex.

"I will do laundry tonight, and tell Grams she needs to start using her psychic powers for good instead of evil." Taylor heard the mirthful laugh of her grandmother, who was no doubt laughing from her perch at the kitchen table listening on speakerphone. "I love you guys, but I'd better—"

"Jesus, Cousins, could you not get any bigger panties? What the hell are they? Did NASA lose a parachute or something?"

Taylor snapped her waistband back into place in record time, turning to glare at the rude incomer.

"Got to go, Mom, love you." Ending the call before her mother could get a word in, she poked Sebastian Brown in the chest and relished the flinch it produced on his smug features. "I don't know, Brown. Maybe you could ask them next time you go in to talk about your issues. What was it again, a probing by little green men in the desert?"

His lips twitched as he leaned against his locker, which of course was directly opposite hers. "That's right, yeah. After they scanned you, they wanted to take someone else just to double-check that not all humans were uptight little know-it-alls."

She pulled a face, jutting her lower lip out at him as she shoved her tired feet into one of the fresh pairs of sneakers she kept in her locker. Last night's pair was currently nestling in the medical waste bin, having been puked on and the recipient of bodily fluids from a boil she'd lanced off a patient in the ER late in her shift. Both courtesy of the same patient, who hated hospitals so much he'd waited till the pain was excruciating before seeking medical help.

That was one of the reasons she would never choose general surgery over cardiac care as a specialty. Too much pus and vomit for her liking. It was also a huge reason why she needed to nail this last part of her internship—to get the spot she'd been working toward for so long. She'd be on a higher salary too, which would certainly help her send more money her family's way. Things were tight in the money department. There would be no fancy underwear in her drawer anytime soon; that was for sure. A life of frugality and coupon clipping for the foreseeable future was a sure thing, but the women in her life had prepared her well. Raised her to be tough and independent.

"So, about those panties..." Sebastian's needling tones assaulted her ears, and she just about resisted the urge to growl at him. Thinking of vomit and excruciating pain, she turned back to face her work nemesis with a stare that would knock a weaker man clean off his feet.

"Finish that sentence, I dare you. My underwear is nothing to do with you, Casanova."

"Casanova? *Moi?*" He gasped theatrically, his hands coming up to his chest in horror. "Don't tell me you believe the chatter around here, Cousins. Gossiping is beneath you."

She grabbed her stethoscope and checked her favorite pen was in her breast pocket before she bothered to reply. She could feel his gaze on her, those brown eyes sparkling with some pithy comeback to her retort. God, he was annoying. Her blood pressure went up whenever he was in her vicinity, and he knew it. He was always saying things that she was thinking before she got them past her lips. Anticipating her moves in the OR like some kind of creepy mind reading wizard. If this was Hogwarts, he would definitely be the Dark Arts teacher. He even had the Snape stare down pat.

The worst thing was, half the time, she could anticipate him too. Know what he was thinking, what his next move would be when treating a patient. In a professional, practical way, it was perfect. Any other situation? Frustrating to the point of making her want to rip her hair out in bunches. A side effect of them constantly working together and circling each other like lions around a carcass, no doubt. Like now, when she knew simply by looking at him that he was holding his breath and just waiting for her to clap back. *Not today, Satan's hellish underling.* Today, she was going to rise above it.

Ready to round, she turned to Selina, who was watching the pair of them with a knowing smirk on her face. She always had that look, no doubt used to them tearing strips off each other by now. When it came to the two of them, Selina's default setting was set to highly amused.

"Ready?" Taylor asked her friend, who closed her book with a nod. She took a few steps so she was almost toe-to-toe with the fellow intern she despised more than she did almost anything else in the world, and grinned when his pupils dilated at her close proximity. "And I don't gossip, Brown. I just read the bathroom walls when I get bored. See you at rounds."

"Can't wait!" he called after her just before the doors swished closed behind them. Selina covered her mouth, and Taylor caught it.

"Don't laugh at him! You just feed the monster!"

"I'm sorry!" Selina soothed, looking anything but apologetic. "But it was pretty funny. I mean, you did flash him."

"I did not!" Taylor screeched, ducking her head when a passing nurse gave them a quizzical look. "I did not," she stage whispered, "and he shouldn't have been looking anyway. He's a jackass of the highest order. I mean, seriously, why do I have to work alongside him all the time?"

"Er…because you are both specializing in cardiothoracic surgery, you compete with each other like it's a blood sport and the gods of fate like a laugh?"

Taylor groaned, and Selina linked arms with her as they headed to the elevator to go to the ER floor.

"Come on, it's not so bad. Once you get one of those residency spots in cardio, you'll be golden. I'll be delivering babies and saving expectant mothers from complications, and you will be rocking the cardiac department. I can already see it now, roomie."

"Oh yeah, sure, like it's that easy. Every intern who wants cardio is vying for a spot here. I mean, aside from Boston and Germany, Vegas is the premier spot for a cardio residency. Just because I'm here in the same hospital doesn't mean that it's set in stone that I will get one of the two spots." She bit the inside of her lip, feeling the familiar rush of stress and fear zip through her body. "I need this, Selina. If I land in another state, even with a relocation package it would still cost me to move, and moving away from my mom? My grandma? It's unthinkable. Grams is already threatening to come out of retirement to help with costs, and Mom only works part-time with her still recovering. If I have to leave… Well, it just can't happen. They deserve to take it easy."

A flash of Sebastian's smug face pervaded her senses. "Even more unthinkable is the thought of Brown getting one of the spots over me. Seriously, I would rather lose to literally anyone else on the planet than him. Can you imagine how much he'd gloat? I've fought too hard not to earn a place now, even if both of us end up staying and I have to put up with him as a resident." She growled at the thought, making Selina giggle. "Ooh! I could strangle him with my stethoscope with a happy smile on my face."

Selina rolled her eyes. "You two are the worst. And best, at that. I swear, watching the two of you bicker all the time makes the long hours almost bearable. I have to say, I'm kind of rooting for you both at this point. It will make residency a lot more fun."

Her pager beeped and she checked it, her face lighting up. "Finally, my laboring mother is at eight centimeters. Got to go! I'll catch you on rounds, okay? Try not to kill any handsome interns while I'm gone."

"I make no such promise," Taylor quipped to her friend's retreating form. "Good luck with the birth!"

Dr. Aisha Ashanda, the intern director of Vegas Valley Hospital, was in her usual no-nonsense mood. Rounds had been as efficient and brutal as ever. Dr. Ashanda was a professional through and through, a top surgeon in her own right, and *the* person to impress. She was also not a fan of the warm and fuzzies, which meant that every intern at the Valley was pretty much terrified and in awe of her in equal measure. Patrick Rowan, the current recipient of her attentions, was practically vibrating in fear.

"Dr. Rowan, since you were five minutes late for my rounds this morning, I assume that you have at least made a note of some of your patients' histories? Given that you forgot this patient's basic details, I suggest that you improve your memory retention. Care to try again on this patient's history?"

The intern being questioned, a squirrely guy who was only interested in plastic surgery, withered under her scrutiny. "I…er… I…"

Poor Patrick. Taylor didn't know him well, given that he was besties with Sebastian, but he wasn't a bad guy. The four of them did tend to gravitate to each other, at least when they were on shift together, which was more down to Selina than anything else. Patrick was a little sloppy, sure, but his heart was in the right place. None of which Dr. Ashanda cared about. She wanted dedicated, perfectionist interns who put the job and the patients above all else.

"Yes and no are complete sentences, Doctor. Why don't you pick one."

"No. Sorry, Dr. Ashanda."

Pushing her black-rimmed glasses farther up her nose, she waved him away. "Thanks for your honesty. To rectify your lack of patient knowledge, you can do the charting today. The nurses are swamped so I'm sure they'll appreciate having a willing lackey. Make sure you get everything signed off with an attending, and they will report back, so please don't embarrass yourself. Or more importantly, me."

Not waiting for an answer, she turned to the other interns, leaving Patrick to slink off with his tail between his legs. "Who wants to present for this patient?"

Sebastian and Taylor spoke at once, reeling off patient details until Dr. Ashanda lifted a hand to silence them both.

"Eager as usual. Dr. Brown, you take this one."

Sebastian nodded, reciting details for a surgery that Taylor worked on last night. She had quite literally done the stitching on his pericardium; Dr. Ashanda had let her close. She'd grown quite attached to this patient, who was a jovial guy in his forties. A keen athlete who had keeled over on a run, almost leaving behind his devoted wife and young son. As she'd told Selina the last time she'd moaned about her skipping their run in favor of a romantic comedy and potato chips in their apartment. Sometimes exercise could be just as dangerous as being a coach potato.

"Hank Anderson, forty-two. Day one post–coronary artery bypass graft, otherwise known as a cabbage. Operation went successfully; minimal bleeding and patient is comfortable. Observation signs are normal and patient is stable and comfortable."

"With a rather neatly sewn up incision site," Taylor added under her breath.

If Sebastian heard her, he didn't let on. Dr. Ashanda looked her way, and she was pretty sure she saw the ghost of a smile on her face. Of course, it could just be wind or something, a tired muscle twitch. Taylor had managed to grab a nap postsurgery but she would bet her last dollar that their mentor hadn't so much as closed her eyes. The woman was a machine, and the best teacher that she could ever hope for. Not only was she the intern director for surgery, but she was also the top cardiothoracic surgeon in the country. People crossed states to be operated on by her, and she picked her own cases to work on. In short, the woman was who Taylor wanted to be. A living, breathing tool for her patients, dedicating her life to her craft.

It made getting that internship all the more important. Taylor would work directly under her if she got the place *and* get to stay near her family. Sure, she might have to move back in with her mom and Grams if the worst happened and Selina didn't get her residency place at the Valley, but her roommate was helping to birth babies and making it look as easy as shelling peas. It was why the two of them had bonded so quickly at the start of their internships. They were cut from the same cloth, even if Selina didn't have the financial stress that Taylor had bearing down on her shoulders.

Selina did have a rather nice apartment close to the hospital, though, courtesy of her family, and it was a nice bonus that Taylor's best friend had a nice home to share with her. With the hours they worked, schlepping home to the Cousins women every night would have been exhausting.

Not to mention the fact that they were a lot, in the nicest way. Her grandmother had sent her a link to Tinder just last week. Which was laughable, because both Grams and Mom had had disastrous relationships with their partners; both women had ended up as single parents. How Grams thought it would work out any different for her granddaughter, Taylor had no clue. Neither of them had dated after Grandad and Dad left, and given that both fathers had left before their child reached double figures, it didn't exactly promote the confidence to bother trying.

Grams and Mom were happy enough just being the three of them. Taylor loved her childhood, aside from the lack of money and Mom getting sick. There were no Prince Charmings on those dating apps, and she was no damsel in distress. She could slay the dragons in her life without a man in tow, just like the women before her. In short, she would rather run down the hospital corridor in her big-girl pants than let someone like that into her life. Given the caliber of the men she spent time with, they would no doubt be a pain in the posterior anyway.

Ever since the first day of her internship, she'd butted heads with Sebastian, and that took enough of her time. She had thought that they might be friends, but seeing him flash his Rolex, charming the nurses like birds in the trees, she'd kept her distance. On that first shift, they'd competed, ribbed each other relentlessly—and that was it. The die was cast. They were similar in a lot of ways, seemed to understand each other. The thing was, they took full advantage of the chink in each other's armor. He was too much like her dad: all confidence and that way with the ladies. She knew the type, and she didn't want anything to do with him or anyone like him.

When Dr. Ashanda spoke again, she realized she'd tuned out and snapped her attention back into place. When she glanced across at Sebastian, he whipped his head down to the floor like there was something highly interesting there. Probably checking that huge ego of his was still attached.

"...to that end, with you all successfully passing your boards, and heading off for a short break before we do this all again on Monday, I just wanted to thank you all for your hard work. I know that this final year has been challenging, but don't lose sight of the end goal." Eyeing each of them in turn, Dr. Ashanda was all assessment. "The residencies that you will undertake in less than a month will be harder still, and wherever you place, they will not accept any kind of slacking off. So," she said and half grinned, which looked oddly unnatural on her usually stoic face, "for once, my advice is to go out there and have some fun."

The interns were looking at her aghast until she added, "Doctor's orders. After this weekend, there will be absolutely no time for fun. So enjoy, my little interns. When your shift is over today, fly, be free—and come back on Monday ready to work."

She departed like a dark queen, leaving everyone behind feeling more than a little shell-shocked by her parting demand.

"Did I just hallucinate that, or did she really mandate that we enjoy ourselves this weekend? I mean, giving us two days off? I can't wait!" *To do my laundry. Do sleep. To finally binge-watch that Netflix show everyone has been talking about for weeks.* Whipping out her phone as she walked down the corridor, Taylor suddenly felt an icy chill at her back.

"Whatcha doing, Cousins, googling *fun*? It's spelled *f-u*—"

"Funny," she responded. "I know a two-word sentence that starts with those letters. Care to venture a guess?" She turned to shoot him one of her stellar glares but was met with a broad chest. *Damn him, being so tall and...wide.* He was like a darn mountain. She craned her neck to meet his ever-knowing smile. "Or...even better, why don't you just go away and torture someone else for a change?"

He scrunched his nose, as though he was truly considering it. "Nah," he chuckled with a shake of his head. "It's far better to torment you instead."

"Whatever." She pushed past him, but he followed in her wake.

"So, who are you messaging? Hot date? I didn't think those apps allowed snarky, caustic members to be let loose on the unsuspecting public. I hope your profile comes with a warning. Poor guys aren't going to know what hit them."

"Like your unsuspecting matches, you mean? I bet you get a discount for being a frequent flyer too. Your reviews must be epic."

He stepped out in front of her so fast she smushed her face in that torso of his. Of course it was hard, muscular. She could practically feel the ripple of each taut asset under her cheek.

"Hey, walk much?" he teased.

She wobbled on her feet, which only made him

chuckle harder as he gripped her upper arms and righted her like she weighed nothing. Seriously, he put her back on her feet like she was a bag of feathers. Which of course annoyed her intensely, because screw him. Mr. Perfect was just too perfect. Too cute, too hot. Too burly and strong. It was hard, having such a specimen of an enemy, and it only served to make her don more armor when she was around him.

Not that he cared of course. No matter how many layers of steel she wrapped herself in, the dude just saw right through it. Like now, when he was watching her with an amused half smile dancing on his lips.

"I ambulate better than you do, Bambi. I don't use the apps either. I told you, just because the nurses bat their eyelashes doesn't mean I entertain them. I'm like you, Cousins. Married to the job, and I am a one-woman type of guy." He narrowed his eyes to match her incensed scowl, then had the audacity to wink.

He actually winked! Who was the god of mischief, Loki? All this guy needed was a pair of horns and he could pass for him any day of the week. *Stop with the superhero comparisons, Taylor. Pull it together.* They continued with their staring contest until his beeper went off. He took one look at it, and his face dropped.

"Aww, who is it?" She teased in a baby voice. "Satan, wanting his minion back in hell?"

"Hank," he uttered in reply, and then the pair of them took off running in tandem, not stopping till they skidded into his room. One of the nurses was doing CPR, but the monitor was one big flat line when she stopped.

"How long has he been down?" Sebastian asked, stepping forward to take over the CPR while Taylor ran to the other side to prepare the defibrillator.

"The monitor went off four minutes ago. When we got here he wasn't breathing. No pulse. We shocked him at two hundred, but there's been no response."

"And all of his observations were fine? He had no sign of infection. Did his bloods come back?"

The nurse shook her head. "All normal. He was talking to me not ten minutes ago, Doctor."

The machine beeped and Taylor dived into action. "Clear!"

Sebastian raised his hands and she placed the paddles on Hank's chest and shocked him. His body jolted, but the whole room had their eyes on the monitor. It registered the shock, and they waited…but the line went flat.

"Charging to two-fifty!" Taylor raised the voltage and the second the monitor beeped, shocked him again. Again, the monitor registered nothing after the shock. "How many rounds of epi has he had?"

"He's maxed out," the nurse at her side said, her face grim.

For the longest few seconds, the team looked down at the patient, knowing that he was too far gone to get back. Taylor went to check the pulse in his neck, and her finger brushed Sebastian's, who was doing the same thing. They locked eyes. She opened her mouth to say something, anything—but nothing came to mind. She'd wracked her medical brain to think of a way to bring their patient back. A procedure they could try to turn back the tide in the direction of living. His operation had gone so well. He had been so healthy before this, had so much to live for. She'd already written his name in her win column.

"Charge again," Sebastian commanded, his voice strong and clear. Taylor met his eye, and the message passed from doctor to doctor. One more shot. One more try, a Hail Mary.

"Doctor, I..." the nurse started, but Taylor nodded and readied the paddles.

"He's right, one more chance. We tried everything else, but Hank deserves one last shot at going home to his family. Charge again."

Both doctors kept their eyes locked on each other, and the second the machine beeped, she raised the paddles. "Clear. Come on, Hank, not today."

The whole team held their breath as Hank's

pale body jolted and dropped back to the bed. The monitors registered the shock once again.

"Nothing." Sebastian's tone was glum. "His heart's too far gone. Must have been a clot. Complications happen, sadly."

Taylor's eyes flashed to his.

"I know that, Brown. Is the attending coming?"

The nurse shook her head. "We related the course of treatment. Dr. Ashanda said you would know what to do."

She didn't want to acknowledge him, but the first thing she did was look at Sebastian. He was already watching her, a grim set to his mouth that she recognized all too well. She knew he was reading her too, and as much as she hated that, losing her patient was far, far worse.

They'd been here before, too many times. Working on a patient and not being able to change the outcome. Failing to chase death away from the person in their hands. They just couldn't save everyone, despite their best efforts. Being the obsessive doctors they were, she knew his expressions by now. Even with the surgical masks on, they spoke to each other through the eyes. She knew he was upset too, about Hank. Was experiencing that same frustrated, powerless feeling currently coursing through her whole body.

Moments like this were the rare occasions where an unspoken trust passed through them. One that lasted till the next traded insult, anyway. For some reason, she got the feeling that their fierce banter was part of his armor too. Protecting something under that chink, like she protected her secrets.

Their eyes met again, and she echoed the sigh that pushed out of his chest as they both turned to look at Hank again, at the flatline on the monitor. They both knew the score. Like Sebastian said, complications postsurgery happened. Sometimes the body was just too far gone, the heart having withstood too much to recover even though all of the signs were strong. They wouldn't know till a postmortem was done, if the family deigned to agree to one.

Dr. Ashanda wasn't at Hank's bedside because she trusted her team and knew that there was nothing that they could have done. In that moment, Taylor thought of his family, who were right now out to get something to eat after waiting for him to come out of surgery mere hours before. They would be back soon, expecting to see him still in bed, recovering and happy to see them. Hank's wife was already worrying about the cost of the surgery; she'd confided in her that much. Now? To lose him anyway? It just felt like a cruel joke.

This part of the job, the patients they thought were saved but death took anyway? They hit the hardest. They made all the studying and obsessing, the attention to every moment of patient care seem futile. It brought back the helpless feeling she'd had in her gut since her mother first got sick. Wishing she could cut out the cancer from her body and save her.

Her mother was lucky, but that feeling had never left. The utterly terrifying certainty that life was not under her control, no matter how hard she worked and how deep she dug her heels in.

"Cousins. Do you need me to do it?" Sebastian's voice was uncharacteristically soft, and the tears that were brimming in the corners of her eyes retreated at the sound. She could handle this. She didn't need to be helped. It went against everything she stood for, even in the rare moments between them like this. She shook her head, pushing her mother out of her head and pulling deep on her steely resolve.

"Time of death, 10:32. Let Dr. Ashanda know. She will want to speak to the family herself."

The nurses nodded, heading off to do the various tasks needed when a patient lost their life. Hank would have to be prepared for the family to see him; paperwork needed to be filed. The admin and procedures of death that were a cruel and necessary part of life. Poor Hank was at rest now, but Taylor knew that his family's pain was only just beginning. Trying to stay professional as her emotions stormed inside her, she pulled off her gloves and threw them into the nearest bin.

When Sebastian caught up with her in the corridor, she was about to lose it. She needed to get out of there, hide in the bathroom for a moment. Have a little cry and then push her feelings down and get back to the job she loved. And hated a little, in this moment. Her mother was firmly on her mind, and for a moment there, all she could see was her in a bed like that. Worrying about the future, the cost of trying to stay alive on top of fighting the horrible, cruel thing that was trying to kill her from the inside out.

Taylor didn't want him of all people to see her like this. He wouldn't understand. How could he? They came from very different worlds. She knew he'd been to all the best schools, had the flashy car. His family would no doubt have the funds to cover the best insurance, a buffer in their bank instead of living paycheck to paycheck. She'd once heard him talking about skiing in France as a kid. The closest she'd been to that was when her mother had fashioned a sledge out of old planks and they'd dragged it up the hill near their house to play together.

She wasn't about to tell Sebastian Brown any of that, and if he made a cutting comment, or worse, tried to console her? She was going to lose it. That moment in there, it had crossed into something they didn't do for each other—beyond the synchronicity they always kept their boundaries. They knew that the other didn't need any help from them. Changing that felt wrong. They kept that stuff well away from their working relationship. She'd come this far on her own. Her family and work were her focus; anything else she just couldn't trust—or waste time on.

"What is it, Brown?"

He didn't say anything for a long moment, his hand running through the hair at the back of his head. "Nothing. I just wanted to tell you, that wasn't your fault back there. I saw the surgery. It went textbook."

She felt her jaw clench tight as she tried to regain control of herself. She didn't need him in her face right now. She knew it wasn't her fault. It didn't make the outcome any easier to swallow. Her eyes were burning from the threat of her unshed tears, and she was damned if she was going to let Sebastian see it of all people.

"I think the family might go for an autopsy, if it helps," he continued.

"Helps? How does that help, Brown? I don't need verification that I didn't mess up. I know I didn't! The whole team worked hard from start to finish, we gave him the best care, and…"

Oh god. It's happening. Her voice had nearly given out on her, and she could feel the thick slab of pain clog up her throat. *No, no, no. Not now.*

"Cousins," he said, his whole demeanor gentle. It was too weird, seeing him all…compassionate like this. His whole manner was strange, unwelcome. It poured fire right into her, drying up any tears that lingered with a loud hiss she swore she could hear in her head.

"Don't, okay. Whatever this is, this nice-guy act? I'm not buying it. God, why are you always in my head, Brown? I don't need you to check up on me, okay? I am a professional, just like you. I don't need consoling, and if I ever did, you would be firmly in the last-man-on-earth category."

Whatever softness she saw on his features disappeared as he took a step back.

"Fine, Cousins. I was just trying to be nice. Like you said, I could tell you were upset. You know, we do have to work together. We might get in each other's heads, but that doesn't mean we can't check up on each other. We worked on Hank together. I get it, losing a patient is hard."

"Again with the obvious. Look, we don't like each other. I don't need your help."

He tutted. "Never said you did. You are a pain in my ass, and I know for a fact it goes both ways."

"Yep. Exactly. So don't play the hero, because it doesn't wash with me. I am a professional. I had a moment. It's over."

"Good."

"Good." She nodded, her feet already moving. "Just stay out of my way today, Brown. Do us both a favor."

She didn't wait for a reply, didn't look back. When she passed the bathroom door, she kept walking right to the nurses' station and picked up the next patient intake file. She was going to work her ass off today and show Sebastian Brown that she didn't need him. She didn't need anyone.

God, she is so...infuriating! She wasn't kidding when she said they were in each other's heads. Sebastian hated that she could read him like a book. About as much as he despised being keyed into her too. When they worked together it was like they were the same person. She was already reaching for an instrument before his fingers twitched half the time. *Maddening even in her efficiency.*

Hank's death was unexpected, but not totally out of the realm of what they dealt with every day. He knew that something else was bothering her, making her even more prickly than usual. Usually he'd just rib her about it, but instead he'd made the stupid mistake of trying to be nice. Obviously a byproduct of losing a patient. He'd lost his senses. She didn't do nice, after all. Not to him, anyway. He meant what he said—she was a pain in his ass.

She clearly thought he had it so easy in life, but she had no clue. No one knew what he'd had to do to get here. He worked just as hard as anyone else in the program. If he and Taylor both got the top spots, he wondered, was this going to be what his residency would be like? Fighting with a woman who was so thorny and independent that she lashed out like a stray cat? She treated him like a playboy, but he was a nerd deep down.

See? You can't read everything about me, Cousins. Not even you bother to get the real me.

He might have money, but it came with a steep price. Taylor might need this residency, but he had to get one of the spots too. It was his next step. It was everything he'd worked for, and finally he would prove that he could make it on his own. That he didn't need anyone's help to make his way in the world.

One thing was for sure—Taylor Cousins was the thorn in his side, and that wasn't going to change anytime soon.

CHAPTER TWO

"PATRICK'S IN FINE form again, I see." Taylor followed Selina's nod across the bar later that night, where Dr. Patrick Rowan was holding court over a bunch of very giggly nurses. "I don't get what they see in him."

"I do," Taylor laughed. "They see a guy who is going to make the big bucks, and will no doubt be in want of a wife. I mean, look at him. He has a button missing on his shirt and he looks like his mother still cuts his hair over the kitchen sink. He's a project all wrapped up in a doctorate."

"Eww." Selina winced, draining the rest of her IPA before sliding out of the booth. "That whole summary made me despair for feminism. Another?"

Taylor looked down at the half pint she was still nursing and drank it down. "Sure. The laundry can wait a little longer."

"Atta girl." Selina grinned, patting her on the shoulder before heading toward Patrick and his groupies.

Taylor checked her phone, sending her mother a quick check-in message before shoving it back into her bag with a sigh. The rest of the shift had been brutal. The ER had been as busy as ever, but when Hank's family had arrived and been ushered into the family room, Taylor had stayed out of the way. Now his wife and kids were left without him, and since the surgery wasn't fully covered by his insurance, they also had a bill to pay. With no life insurance in place, it was another blow to the family who now had to navigate life without the person they loved in it.

It had been the same with her mother. Had she been able to afford life insurance with critical coverage, they would have been a lot better off. With their health insurance policy not covering a lot of the costs, every hospital visit had been even worse to bear, knowing that the invoices were racking up.

Insurance was the part of the job that Taylor hated the most, especially after losing a patient. The whole system was crazy, how people got treatment and lived and others didn't because of their circumstances in life. She and her family were living proof of the damage it could cause, and how it affected the patient even after they survived whatever tried to kill them in the first place. The whole thing was depressing, and Taylor felt bone-tired.

The bar was a few blocks from the hospital,

and a regular haunt for a lot of the medical staff who worked there. It wasn't quite the Vegas glitz, not quite a dive bar—it kind of ran a fine line in between, which was probably why it was so popular among her colleagues. It was also the last place she wanted to be right now, but Selina had taken one look at her at the end of their shift and wordlessly dragged her to the locker room to make her get changed.

"Hi."

Taylor looked up to see a man standing in front of the booth, a beer in his hand.

"Er…hi." She flashed him a smile she didn't feel and nodded toward the bar. "Sorry, this booth's taken. My friend just went to get drinks."

The man, a short guy wearing a hockey jersey from a team she didn't recognize and a sheepish smile, laughed awkwardly. "Well, actually I was just coming over to see if I could buy you a drink. You were looking a little sad, sitting here all alone."

"Sad? Really." That was a pickup line? No wonder she didn't bother dating. What did this guy do? Search for lone depressed-looking women? Eyeing him properly for the first time, she could see he was a little drunker than she first thought. A hockey game was on the big screen in the corner, so he was obviously out with the guys on a bit of a session. "Well, I'm fine. Thanks for asking."

She pointedly looked behind him, hoping that

Selina was going to rock up with their drinks and this guy would shuffle off back to his buddies. He reminded her of her father, and that was never a good look on anyone. She didn't remember a lot about the man who hadn't bothered to raise her, but she recalled the smell of alcohol on his breath. Him missing work to follow his sports team around with his buddies, leaving her mother to hold the fort back home with whatever meager money he didn't spend. Being with a man like that would be a death sentence to the life she wanted. Being with any man, for that matter. All they brought was trouble, and she didn't have room for that in her busy schedule.

Oblivious to Taylor's trip down memory lane, the inebriated hockey fan was not handling her dismissal well.

"You know, you could be nicer. I was only offering a drink. You don't have to be such a—"

"Hey, honey." Sebastian slid into the booth right next to her and draped his arm around her shoulders. "Sorry I took so long. The Golden Knights fans are pretty happy their team are winning—the bar's packed." Without missing a beat, he turned to the rude drunk and pulled a sympathetic face. "I'm sure your luck will turn around at some point, just not today. Have a good night."

The drunk guy and Taylor both blinked at each other, and Taylor watched in shock as he muttered something about shooting the puck and shuffled off back to his friends. Selina, smirking her head off, slid into the booth at her other side, Rowan carrying a tray of drinks following right behind.

"That was hilarious," Patrick laughed. "You dissed his team and pointed out his striking out in one sentence."

Selina passed her a beer, and it was only when she moved to take it that she realized Sebastian was still cuddling her. She shoved him off, making her friends laugh. Sebastian didn't join in.

"I didn't need your help," she spit. "I was handling it just fine."

Sebastian took a bottle from the tray with a shrug. "Never said you weren't."

"Well, you implied it when you came in all alpha."

"Alpha? My team is owning his on the ice, and I can't do with rude drunks." His brow quirked at Patrick. "What do you say, Pat? Was that alpha, or beta?"

Patrick tore his eyes away from a couple of girls whose gaze had followed him from the bar. "Alpha, definitely. You could have peed on her, of course, but that would have been a little too obvious." He cast a glance toward the now-baying hockey fans, who were drowning each other in beer as they sang "Sweet Caroline" at the top of their lungs. "I will never understand the whole alpha thing anyway. I thought women wanted a bit more these days than to be dragged to some man cave."

Selina bopped him on the nose and passed him one of the eight shots sitting on the tray. "Poor little beta. Drink up, you'll feel better." Patrick gingerly took it, looking like he was anything but happy to not be an alpha. "Come on, you guys, we need to celebrate!"

"Do we?" Taylor moaned, taking hers and ignoring the way that Sebastian's thigh touched hers as he leaned over to get his. "We lost Hank today. The whole operation went like a dream, but he's still dead, right? His family is screwed now."

"Screwed how?" Sebastian asked.

"Not everyone can afford life and health insurance," Taylor sneered, shooting daggers at him. "What about the financial costs, huh? The stress, the worry? His surgery was thousands of dollars, and for what?"

"The financial side of medicine is beyond our control, Cousins." Sebastian's tone was as cold as she had ever heard it, his jaw tight with tension. "That's down to the insurance companies, not us. We can advise our patients the best we can. Surgery costs money, and someone has to pay for it. I don't like it either, believe me, but you can't fight the system."

"Exactly," Taylor sighed, her mother's face flashing in her head again. She could still remember her grandmother googling her meager jewelry collection to see how much it was worth. The women had never had much, and the thought of them losing what they did have was always the motivating factor behind all Taylor's decisions. "Sure, someone has to pay. But the system sucks for the patients and families who have to go through it. You just don't get it."

There was a stunned silence around the booth, a sharp contrast to the other revelers. She could feel Sebastian's eyes on her but refused to look his way. She'd said too much, and this piece of her, the angry, frustrated side, was the part that she especially wanted to keep away from him. She needed to stay mad, to keep that shield of hers firmly up. Especially around him, because lately all he seemed to do was sneak past it. He was too observant, too all-seeing.

She didn't need some man in her head, in any capacity. Especially not someone who got under her skin so easily. It was his worst quality, and the longer they spent together the harder it was to navigate. So they did what they always did when the tension was so thick a scalpel would be hard pressed to penetrate it. They stared and glared at each other. She tried to make the vein in his forehead bulge and avoid being drawn into how good-looking he was. All while he tried to stare her down with those big stupid brown eyes of his, while his brows varied from downright scowl to shocked audacity. How many hours had they done this? At this point, she knew his face as well as her own. She could draw it from memory. The noise from the bar melted away, till it was just the two of them in that booth. The world.

It was Patrick who broke the tension.

"Well," he said, pulling out his wallet and flashing a credit card. "In that case, there's only one thing for it."

Selina eyed his card, a curious look on her face. "What? Get drunk on your daddy's money?"

Patrick waggled his brows, looking at each of them in turn. "Hey, I work too, you know. We need to go out, live it up. Get drunk? No. Not just drunk. Vegas drunk. I'm talking hit the strip on a full-on assault. Gambling, shots, the whole nine yards. My treat."

"Your father's, you mean," Selina teased but Patrick looked entirely unabashed.

"Well, he did sort of give me a bonus, for getting this far in the internship. Is that bad?"

"No, honey," Selina giggled. "It might be the shots, but I think using your bonus to go all out might just be the best idea you've ever had."

Patrick looked so happy, it reminded Taylor of a toddler who had his artwork put on the fridge. Hell, his parents probably did that. God only knew that the Cousins' fridge was laden down with her photos and achievements.

"Thanks, Lina." He grinned, puffing out his chest. "So, Vegas? All-out fun and debauchery?"

Sebastian groaned. His "Pat, come on" was met with a wide grin as Patrick nodded at them like an eager little Labrador.

"I'm not in the mood," Taylor moaned, but Selina elbowed her in the ribs. "Hey!"

"Sorry, but you kind of deserved that one." Selina patted Patrick on the head like she was his happy master and he blushed with pride. "I never thought I would say this, but Dr. Rowan here has a point. We are off all weekend! That never happens, and we are sitting here in a crappy bar moaning about the health care system and watching other people have fun! Come next week, we are going to be right back at it. Living for work, studying. Dr. Ashanda literally told us to get out there and have some R and R. We live in Sin City like angels, and I think we owe it to ourselves, and Hank," she said with a pointed stare at Taylor, "to celebrate life while we can. To get out there and actually enjoy being alive for once. Patrick here has it covered, right?"

He was already pulling up hotel bookings on his phone.

"Yep. I have a buddy who works at the Bellagio, owes me a favor. We could get a couple of rooms, hit the tables, see a show!" He turned his screen to flash them a photo of a Barry Manilow tribute singer. Selina shot him a withering look in return.

"Everything but the show. Seriously. You put

octogenarians to shame." She turned to Sebastian, who was looking like he'd rather be anywhere else but party to this insane plan. "Come on, Sebastian, we have no ties. No work. It's one night, let's turn this day right around!"

"I don't know," he sighed, giving Taylor a quick side-eye. "It could be good, or it could be the worst night ever. There might be actual blood drawn, and I'm not talking about with a needle."

Patrick made a sound like a whining puppy. "Come on, dude! It's Vegas, baby! Let's see it for once, instead of the drab hospital walls! You can call a truce for one night, right? Taylor?"

Taylor was still thinking about how she could cry off, knowing that she had no excuse other than washing her underwear. A hit TV series bingeathon was not going to buy her a ticket out of this, and Selina knew as well as she did that this weekend was a blank space in her calendar. She was about to try anyway when Patrick let out a triumphant whoop at whatever he saw on Sebastian's face. When her head snapped to his, he just threw her a what-are-you-going-to-do shrug, and her stomach dropped to the floor of the booth.

"You really want to do this?" Taylor asked. Sebastian, to her horror, looked like he was buying in to this. "We can't just go all out like that. We haven't planned it."

"Oh yeah? What else are you going to do, wait

for another drooling hockey fan to come bother you? Go home to finish your crochet blanket?"

"No, but—"

"As much as I can't believe I'm saying this," Sebastian argued, "Patrick is onto something. We lost Hank today. It was tough, right? We're all at a loose end. Everyone else we know is either sleeping or working." He tapped his lips with his index finger. "While you annoy the hell out of me, Cousins, I'm willing to put up with you for the sake of having some fun for once."

Selina and Patrick both whooped in delight, getting to work on Patrick's phone and ignoring Taylor's whimpered pleas.

Sebastian leaned in close, fixing her with a challenging look. "Come on, Granny Panties, it's one night. Have some fun with us."

She opened her mouth to say no. She really did. She didn't need to justify herself to him, let alone anyone else. She could just tell him, right here right now, that she wasn't going to spend some wild night out with the bane of her existence, even if their friends were with them as a buffer. Having to put up with him at work was bad enough. He was under her skin so much she dreamed about the guy. She should just leave. Right now, she could hail a cab and go and do the laundry she needed to do. She could sleep, and rest.

The trouble was, Sebastian Brown was not only

the most annoying man on planet Earth, but he was also the one man who knew exactly what to say to push every single one of her buttons. Like now, when he said the fatal words that changed the course of their weekend.

"What are you waiting for? A sign from above? It's one night. We can put up with each other for that long. Come on. Live a little. I dare you."

Aghast, she looked at Selina and Patrick, but they were no help. The pair of them looked like a couple of bobbleheads, all big grins and exaggerated nods. Sebastian was already smiling like he'd won the big prize when she locked eyes with his and said, "Hope you're ready, Brown, because it's on."

CHAPTER THREE

TAYLOR WISHED SHE'D only woken up the morning after with a stinking hangover and a mouth that felt like she'd licked the bottom of a birdcage. That was bad enough, but she had far, far bigger issues to worry about. Like the wedding ring on her finger, the one that was definitely not there last night when she first hit the Vegas strip. When she came to, lying flat on her stomach with her hand in front of her and the early-morning Vegas skyline staring back at her through the open curtains, it was the first thing her very dehydrated and confused brain processed through her optical nerves. *Why the heck do I have a ring on?*

For a second, she stared at it as though it would disappear like a desert mirage, but nope. There it was. A solid gold ring, right there on her wedding finger like a telltale bleeding heart. *What the hell happened last night? Did I pull off a jewelry heist I don't recall?* She tried to think, but her memory bank was soaked in alcohol and definitely not cooperating with her efforts of trying to remember...well, anything. Everything was a blur of color and laughter, topped off with the familiar sense of dread you woke up with after a heavy night of partying. The certainty that something had happened, and her brain was trying to gauge how much she could cope with on top of the hangover.

She never drank like that. Ever. The number of fruity drinks she'd partaken of last night was one she had never surpassed before and never would again if this was the outcome. Flashes of the night before came screaming back at her as she scanned the unfamiliar hotel room surroundings. Her, drinking with the other interns on the strip. Selina. dancing with her on a darkened dance floor. Sebastian, coming along with his teasing and his dares. The pair of them, having some kind of dance-off while a crowd cheered them on. Patrick, falling over on the strip, dropping his fries and moaning that he was so hungry that the five-second rule should be able to be enforced. Selina, managing to convince him not to pick his food up off the floor and taking him to a burger van. Sebastian, daring her to drink that Day-Glo shot. Sebastian, tipping her back and kissing her hard—

Oh god. *What the heck was that? Delete.* That didn't happen, right? She could never be drunk enough to kiss Sebastian Brown. There wasn't enough alcohol in Vegas to make that image a possibility. She blinked hard, as though she could reboot her gray matter. More images came loose, and she reached for them with trepidation.

Sebastian, laughing as an Elvis impersonator read from a book. The same Elvis telling them to smile as he took a photo of them, Sebastian's arms wrapped tight around her as they both said cheese to the camera. Sebastian's hand in hers as she pushed a circle of gold over his thick knuckle.

No. I didn't. We didn't. No.

Sebastian, pinning her against the hotel room door she was currently looking at in shocked disbelief. Sebastian, his eyes filled with lust as he muttered in her ear, "You're so wet for me, wifey." Sebastian, dipping his head to lick down her stomach and take off her—

"No, no, no." Peeking under the duvet, she squeaked when she confirmed her own nakedness. And what looked like a purpling hickey on her upper chest. "Damn it!"

Christ, my head. Who is shouting? "Hey," Sebastian protested from under the duvet. *Whose bed? Am I at the hotel?* "Inside voices. Please."

The loud woman screamed, jumping about a foot off the bed. Pain bore into his skull like a craniotomy drill.

"Arrggghh! What the—"

He pulled the duvet off his head, noticing a hickey as his bare chest was exposed to the air.

Taylor? Oh. God. A flash of her beneath him last night popped into his head, and he adjusted the duvet around his lower half. *Nope.* He'd dreamed about her before, but never naked. They didn't do anything, right? His memory was still dulled from the tequila it had been bathed in last night.

"What are you doing here?" His voice was still thick with sleep. Husky. "Where's Patrick?"

"I don't know! Selina was supposed to be in here with me! What are you doing here?" She didn't remember either? All signs pointed to the obvious, but he decided to play it dumb, just for now.

"You look naked, Cousins. Why the hell are you naked in my room?"

"Yeah?" It came out as a breathy squeak as she pulled the covers around herself tighter. Not before he spotted a red mark above the swell of her breast. "Well, check yourself out."

His eyes bulged and she squirmed as he lifted the covers up and looked down at himself. Yep, that was definitely a matching hickey. Another image jumped into his head, one where her nails were running down his abs as she slowly rode him till he groaned and pulled her down to his mouth by gripping the nape of her neck. *Oh god, stop.*

"Well," he murmured, feeling as confused as she looked. "This is not how I expected the night to go."

She held up her left hand. "Check out your ring finger."

"What?" He lifted his hand from the quilt, and there it was. A matching gold ring to the one on her finger. It was unavoidable. Unthinkable. "Oh my god. Elvis." He swallowed hard. "I remember Elvis."

"Yep. I remember him too. And that's not the most disturbing thing I remember."

"Jesus. I can't believe this. We had sex." *Great sex, judging from what fragments were coming back.*

"Yep."

"Energetic, sweaty sex."

"Yes."

"You bit me."

"You bit me too!" She lowered the cover just enough to show him her twin injury. "This can't be happening."

"Too late for that." He started to play with his ring, remembering how he'd linked fingers with hers as he thrust into her. How she'd moaned and kissed him like she was starved for his touch. It made his head swim. "We got married and consummated."

"Uh-huh." She sank down onto the pillows. He followed suit, feeling so out of sorts that holding his head up right now felt like too much effort.

"We consummated. A lot, from what I can piece together."

"Indeed."

"Which means no annulment. We'll have to get divorced. Oh god, this is bad. We got married on a dare, Cousins." *My dare. What was I thinking? I really lost my head last night.*

"Oh my god, that's right! You dared me, after we did that run along the strip!" She looked mad, but he was frustrated enough at himself for the both of them. Not that he was going to admit it.

"The race that I won, yeah. I remember now. That little quickie wedding chapel. We were so drunk, you'd think Elvis would have stopped us."

"Oh sure," she scoffed. "Because that's what Vegas is known for, good sober decision-making. Who dares someone to get married anyway? This is your fault!" He sat up, and she pulled the covers tighter as he scanned the room. "What are you doing?"

"Looking for the shotgun I used to force you up the aisle, Cousins, what else? It might have been my dare, but you agreed to it." His eyes fell on the table at the other side of the room. "Close your eyes a sec, okay?"

He left the bed the second he saw her eyes close. He needed to take charge of this, and getting away from her naked body and the scent on their sheets wasn't a bad idea either. His body was recalling their night with gusto, and he needed to hide the evidence.

Getting dressed, he brought up a web search

on his phone. "So, I was right. We can't annul the marriage—it will have to be a divorce. They've really been cracking down on quickie annulments lately. Luckily we both live in this state, so we can file here and get the ball rolling next week." When she didn't say anything, he looked up from his phone. "Taylor, are you even listening to me?"

She sat up in bed, but for once he couldn't figure out what she was thinking. It bothered him. A lot. This whole thing was a lot, and he wished he knew what she thought of it. Of last night. *Get a grip, Seb. What are you expecting, a performance review?*

"Yeah, I heard you. I'm just processing. Also, calling me Taylor is weird."

"Okay." He scratched a hand down his five-o'clock shadow. "What would you prefer, wifey? Ball and chain? My worse half?"

"You know," she snipped, doing that nose-scrunching thing of hers. "I always thought my husband would be funnier than this. Not that I ever wanted one!"

"Oh really?" He tapped a few times on his screen and hit the call button. "Well, I didn't plan to get hitched either, FYI." The call went to voicemail, and he heard Patrick's chipper message. "Damn it, he's not answering."

"Yeah, well. He's probably with Selina in the other hotel room." Her face dropped. "Oh god. Patrick and Selina. Do you think they know?"

Sebastian shook his head. "I don't know. I don't remember them being there in the chapel, and I think they would have stopped us." He pursed his lips. "Well, maybe not Patrick, but Selina would have, I'm sure. One of them would have, surely?"

He huffed out a sigh of relief as he scrolled through his phone. "There's nothing on social media, mine or Patrick's—nothing about us, anyway." His brows dropped into a confused frown. "He did post a photo of some squashed fries on the sidewalk though. You might want to check yours and Selina's in case. The last thing we need is this getting out. No one can know about this. With a bit of luck we can keep this whole thing between the four of us. You know what Dr. Ashanda's like about doctors having messy personal lives. Remember that intern whose girlfriend screamed at him for working late? He was transferred, and that was nothing compared to this. We can't let this…mistake wreck our residencies, right? The hospital is a gossip mill for stuff like this."

"Oh god," she groaned. "This is an actual nightmare." She got out of bed, wrapping the sheet around her as she paced the room while he tried not to look at the creamy skin of her shoulders. The skin he'd licked and nibbled just hours earlier. He could still taste her on his tongue. "This is exactly what I didn't want. I haven't put a toe out of line this whole time. I've sacrificed time with my mother, my grandmother, a sex life—"

She's spiraling, and I know how to get her to stop.

"Well, you can cross that one off the list after last night." She whirled around and got in his face. *Whoops. Maybe not.* "Okay, okay! Sorry, too soon." He held out his hands in surrender, the phone screen lit up with something that made her spiral all over again. "What?"

She grabbed his phone-holding hand, staring at the screen in disbelief. "Brown, what the hell is that? Did you not see this?"

The screen showed a photo of them. They were curled up in bed together, bare shoulders covered by the sheets. She was lying in his arms, wrapped in his embrace, and they were kissing. She looked…blissful, happy. When she looked at Sebastian, she looked as disconcerted as he felt.

"I…er…think we took it last night." He didn't miss the sudden blush that filled her cheeks. "You might want to check your phone too."

She almost tripped on the sheet in her haste to find her phone, which was sporting the same photo as the home screen. At least her social media was clear. The last photo she'd uploaded was one of her and Selina when they went to the beach, and that was a while ago. Selina had uploaded one from last night, but it was of Patrick, looking decidedly sad while he held up a lone fry.

There were a bunch of missed calls from her mother, Selina and Patrick. Her mother had only called once, earlier that morning, but the calls and texts from their friends told a story. They had been looking for the pair of them and judging by the grammar and spelling of their messages, they hadn't been in a fit state last night either. Her mother would be calling again soon, as she always did. She was going to be asking questions, and Taylor had no answers to give her. What would she say? *Sorry, Mom, I didn't answer your call because I woke up married to my nemesis. Oh, and apparently we had a lot of sex too. Hot, steamy, life-changing sex.*

From what she could remember, Sebastian Brown knew how to please a woman. Which only infuriated her further. She'd been so reckless, so stupid. Pushing down her panic, she kicked the logical side of her take-charge brain into gear.

"Okay, so we need to get tested too."

Sebastian's frown was immediate. "We used condoms, judging from the wrappers scattered around, but we can do that if you like. Are you worried about something?"

She bit at her lip. "Well, I'm clean. I take the pill. It's not like I was dating anyone, but—" She had no idea what he did in his spare time. He was gorgeous, by any measure. The nurses definitely thought so, and she teased him about it, didn't she?

"I don't date either, for the record. I told you, just because the nurses try their luck doesn't mean I do anything. I'm clean. I got tested a few months ago and I haven't been with anyone in a long time." He huffed loudly. "Last night was a first for me too."

She didn't know what to say. What to think. *What had gotten into them last night?* They hated each other, but last night…well, that wasn't hate. She opened her mouth to say something, to try to make sense of things, but he was already turning away, saying, "Look. This was obviously a big mistake."

"Obviously," she muttered, trying to shake the thought of them wrapped around each other. "We need a plan. To keep a lid on this, before we both lose what we've worked so hard for."

"Agreed." Sebastian nodded. "I'll do damage control with Patrick, and we'll get this whole thing straightened out before anyone gets a whiff of it. You ask Selina to keep it quiet on your end. I have a lawyer I can call. I'll get the ball rolling. Keep your phone on, okay?" He paused in front of the marriage certificate, and she saw his eyes fall on the photo next to it. "I'll take this. We'll need it to file the paperwork." He gritted his teeth together. "We stick to the plan. Radio silence on the whole weekend. It's kind of my fault anyway. I dared you, right?"

Taylor should feel better, but she didn't. As drunk as she was last night, she'd done this. Willingly. For a dare. She'd been just as hungry for him as he had been for her—she couldn't deny that. She'd risked everything she'd worked for in a single night, and now she had to deal with a divorce on top of everything else?

This was a nightmare. HR would have a fit if anyone found out. They had strict policies on relationships in the workplace. After a few too many bed-hopping incidents, there were strict rules in place. Professional boundaries had to be clear—which meant no drunken hook-ups with your colleagues. Marriage was an exception of course, but she would rather cut off her hands than have anyone know about their quickie wedding.

"Brown, I took the dare. You didn't force me. As much I hate this, it was fifty-fifty."

His brown eyes searched hers. "It was?"

She nodded, feeling exposed under his gaze like never before. "Yes. We both have a lot to lose here. It serves neither of us to have this get out, and as much as we don't like each other—well, it's done. We need to do damage control, right now. Before work on Monday."

"Right. We work together on this, till it's over. Whatever happens with the residencies, we don't interfere with each other's careers."

She half smiled. "Brown, I would kill you if you tried."

He smirked, but it didn't last. "Okay. Well, we need to get out of here. Get to our friends before they have a chance to let it slip out. I'll…er… speak to you before Monday. I'll call you once I get Patrick gagged and bound."

When the door closed behind him minutes later, she sagged with relief. And something else she couldn't quite place. In the course of one night, everything had changed. Her carefully constructed and organized life was tattered, ripped at the seams. She didn't have time for this, for some secret divorce. She'd messed up and done the one thing she had resolved never to fall foul off. She'd gotten involved with a man for one stupid night, hours even—and now look! Work would be a nightmare, wondering when and if their secret was going to explode in their faces. Dr. Ashanda was a woman who didn't like distracted interns. She wanted the best professionals in her department, not…this.

And with Sebastian Brown, of all people. Her new husband was the most infuriating person on the planet. He had not only got under her skin, but he'd also seen and touched almost every naked inch of it. She had to live with that knowledge now, the new side of him she'd never even thought about before. She had to work with him after this, had to compete with him for the residency positions, but now she was secretly married to him too? How was that even going to work? Would she have to tick a different box now when she filled out a form? Single, married, divorced?

Oh god, she was going to be a divorcée, like her mother and grandmother before her. She'd tried so hard not to get trapped in the family curse. She was so mad at herself, so disappointed. She'd watched her mother's life get worse because of a man. Had heard the stories from her grandmother. She was going to be different, the first in their family to succeed on her own. The first to become a doctor, to be financially independent and debt free. The person to finally make the Cousins women truly secure and happy. She couldn't afford to have things fall apart now, not when she was so close.

Her mother and grandmother would go crazy if they knew. She'd talked about Sebastian enough for them to dislike him intensely. If she had to tell them she'd had some kind of passion-fueled wedding night in Vegas with said enemy, her mother was going to think she'd finally lost the plot from working too hard for too long. The thought of it exhausted her.

This marriage of theirs had to stay secret. It had to stay as what it was, a stupid mistake due to their ridiculous competitive streak escalating under the influence of the bright, seductive lights of Vegas. A blip on her otherwise straight trajectory in life. People made mistakes, right? Granted, this was a doozy, but they happened. Vegas was known for mistakes and quickie weddings that didn't last. She was just another person to lose themselves in the moment. She might laugh about it one day. Hopefully when she was a successful cardiac surgeon at the Valley, and Sebastian Brown was just a memory. This was manageable. Totally.

He had the marriage certificate. He was going to sort it out. Hopefully it wouldn't cost too much to file for divorce, given that their marriage was less than a day old and they wouldn't exactly be splitting assets. Her savings would take a hit though, which made her feel sick to her stomach all over again. She needed every penny to live on and pay off her mother's medical bills from her cancer treatment. Her residency spot was, if anything, even more crucial now. Having to leave Vegas and work elsewhere was just not an option, financial or otherwise.

The photo on the table caught her eye, and her shaking fingers reached for it. Elvis was there, grinning at the camera. Sebastian looked as handsome as ever, worse luck. A little more twinkly eyed than usual, his smile wide and free. She looked at the image of her, smushed up to him, and her breath caught. She looked so different. So unlike the reflection that she saw in the mirror every day. In the photo, she looked…relaxed.

Sure, alcohol had something to do with it, but it was more than that. They didn't look like enemies.

"We look like an actual couple," she murmured, taking in every detail. Feeling her headache coming back with a vengeance, she got dressed quickly and tried to call Selina again. It went straight to voicemail, and Patrick didn't answer. *Great.* She wondered if they had hooked up too. They had been getting pretty flirty the night before. Maybe she wasn't the only one who had woken up with a strange bedfellow.

Leaving Selina a message asking her to call her back, she picked up the photo and the ring boxes and headed downstairs to hail a cab. She needed to get a shower, take some tablets for her hangover and hide from the world for a while. Regroup.

"Hey, Mom," she trilled from the back of the cab. "Sorry I missed your call."

"No problem, honey, your grams and I were just up baking. Figured you might be sleeping late or something. You get your washing done?"

Nope, and now I have a ton of fresh dirty laundry to keep under wraps.

"That's the plan for today. I actually went out with Selina and some of the other interns last night. Kind of a celebration for the end of the internships."

"Oh, that's nice honey. Did that boy go?"

That boy. That was how the Cousins women referred to her new husband. A flash of a naked Sebastian moving above her slammed into her brain.

"Er…yeah. He was there."

"That's a shame, but I guess you do work together pretty closely. Did he behave?"

You feel so good, Taylor. Christ, you smell good. I never knew you would feel like this.

"Yes!" she squeaked, earning her an odd look from the driver. "Yes, he behaved. Selina and I kind of kept to ourselves, you know."

"That's my girl. Always doing the right thing. I hope you managed to let your hair down a little though. You work so hard. You deserve a little reckless fun now and then."

As the cab got closer to home, Taylor sunk lower in her seat. "Oh, you know me, Mom. I'm all about the reckless fun. I gotta go, okay? I'll call you later. Save me some cookies."

"Of course, sweetie. You have a nice weekend, okay? No stress."

Looking down at the ring that was still on her finger, she almost laughed out loud.

"Sure, Mom, no stress. Love you both."

"Love you too, baby. Send our best to Selina too."

"Will do." *When I get hold of her.* She had to tell someone what happened. Maybe by saying it out loud, she could start to make sense of it.

Her best friend would help her. She was a levelheaded, educated woman. *Who am I kidding? My bestie is going to laugh her head off and make popcorn before insisting on hearing every tiny detail.*

Later, when she was back in their comfy apartment, she almost wished that Selina had gone missing. Or been involved in a steamy sexathon of her own with Patrick Rowan. Sadly, neither was the case, and she was busy sitting on the couch beside her. Taylor was mostly observing her choking on laughter as they ate enough pizza, dough balls and ice cream to put a competitive eater to shame. *I knew it. Adult rationality has well and truly left the building.*

"Chew much? If you could stop laughing at my train wreck of a life, I would be grateful."

Selina grabbed a napkin to wipe a blob of tomato sauce from her chin. "I'm sorry, but married? I swear, this is the best weekend of my life! What did you say when you woke up next to him?"

"Well, I didn't ask him about a honeymoon, did I? He was as shell-shocked as I was." She ripped a dough ball in half, ignoring the greasy garlic that coated her fingers. She wasn't going to be kissing anyone anytime soon, was she? Maybe she should make garlic part of her daily diet. Ward off any future accidental husbands. "I don't know how this happened."

Selina waggled her brows. "Oh, I have a theory on that one."

"Does it involve tequila?"

"Yep, but you can't blame the alcohol alone for this one." When Taylor shot her a questioning look, she laughed again. "Come on, Tay. You two have been butting heads for so long, this was bound to happen. The sexual tension between you two was palpable. I can smell the pheromones in the air when you two are around each other. I'm surprised you haven't set off the smoke detectors."

"Sexual tension? You're crazy! We despise each other!"

"The opposite of love isn't hate, it's indifference. You were definitely not indifferent to each other. I mean come on, you guys not only got married, but you had sex. Alcohol is not a lobotomy. It lowers impulse control and inhibitions, sure. It increases risk-taking too. Plenty of people have regretted their actions after a night on the sauce, but getting hitched and sucking face? I'm sorry, but that's not hatred."

"Right, but it doesn't mean some secret lust is going on here." It just didn't happen like that. Random marriages borne out of some kind of repressed yearning. She loved a rom-com as much as the next girl, but a spade was a spade, and a movie wasn't real life. "Look at my mom and dad, they were total opposites and they got married and made me. And that car crash was done sober, with planning and forethought. This is not anything more than a huge mess, just like most of their marriage. I swear, they became less themselves the longer they were together, and before he walked out altogether my dad checked out completely. Romance is a trope, Sel, not a healthy life choice."

Selina's snort made her feel silly. "Oh, come on. Your parents are different. They didn't work together so closely and fight like Tom and Jerry for one thing. I swear, I half expect you two to bring out weapons when you go at each other. I think that there's more to it than you think. Sometimes, when drink is involved it brings out a person's true feelings."

"Like wanting to get married by a bad Elvis impersonator? No way. Not a chance. I was mortified when I woke up with him, naked might I add, and I could tell he felt exactly the same. He jumped out of bed and was googling annulments as soon as his eyes opened."

She hung her head, remembering the sight of a panicked, half-naked Sebastian in the hotel room. "I mean, it's not like I expected him to be happy about waking up like that, but you should have seen him. He was just as freaked out as I was, believe me." She looked at her phone, which had lit up with yet another call from Sebastian.

"He's calling again. It might be about the divorce." Selina nudged the phone closer to her. "Answer it! You can't talk about this stuff at work, and you'll have to face him come Monday anyway."

Taylor watched the phone call end, and another message pop up. Selina was right; she should just answer and deal with it, but she just couldn't bring herself to speak to him. More and more of that night had come back to her, and she didn't know how to feel about it. They had been so romantic with each other, so hot for the other's touch. It was too weird, thinking about seeing him at work again and acting normal. She needed the rest of the weekend to get over this blip, to get her head straight. On Monday, she'd deal with it. They'd file the paperwork, get the marriage stuff done with and then she could just forget about it. All of it.

She wasn't ready to face up to the reality yet. Too much was already swirling around in her head. Work was normality. It was what she knew, where she thrived. Speaking to Sebastian on the phone was just one more weird thing she didn't need in her life.

Space. That was what she needed. And time, to get her game face back on and not think about his deep, sultry voice in her ear. At work, facing

Sebastian Brown was just another day at the office, right? It would be fine. Everything would be fine once they were all back in the reality of the Valley. If it was urgent, he'd leave a message.

"No," she said. "I don't want to speak to him right now. His lawyer surely won't work the weekend anyway, and it's not like the courts are open to file."

Selina looked about as convinced as she felt. "Okay, if you're sure, but it's not like you to hide from things."

"I'm not hiding! I just…need a minute to process, that's all. It's already weird when I talk to my mom. I feel guilty for lying to her and Grams, I'm not ready to deal with…you know." *His voice. The thought of how it felt when he whispered to me in the dark.* "Him. It's not like we speak on the phone. It's weird—and I've had enough of that for a lifetime, let alone a weekend. I just don't need to be chatting away to my—"

Selina waggled her brows suggestively. "Your hot doctor husband?"

"You're not funny, Sel. Besides, you spent the night with Patrick. You sure there's nothing to tell there? You looked like you were having fun."

Selina's snort was all mocking. "Oh yeah, we had a wild night. I was pretty drunk. He did look after me though. You know Patrick, he's like an obedient Labrador. Big, dopey, harmless. You want another slice?"

Taylor looked at the box and patted her already full belly. "Nope. I won't get into my scrubs next week if I eat and drink any more."

Selina shot her a cheeky wink. "Well, you married folk tend to let themselves go eventually, I heard. Might as well embrace it."

Taylor flicked a piece of pizza crust at her. "Not funny!"

CHAPTER FOUR

"WHAT WERE YOU THINKING? I thought you would have had my back, man. Seriously." Patrick blanched at his question, which only made Sebastian's mood darker. "Where were you anyway? We were supposed to stick together!" They were standing in the cafeteria, grabbing a coffee before their first shifts back started, and he was spiraling. He hadn't seen or heard from Taylor since they left each other at the hotel, and his calls had gone unanswered so far.

"What do you mean? I didn't know where you two had gone! Selina was pretty blasted, so we stopped by some bush or other so she could vomit while you two were arguing about some kind of race. When we came to find you, there was no sign of either of you and you didn't answer your phones. Selina was hugging one of the shrubs at this point, so I took her back to our room and slept on the bathroom floor while she hugged the toilet bowl. We just figured you were still out, not declaring your love for each other in front of the

King of Rock and Roll." A guffaw erupted from him, which set Sebastian's teeth on edge.

This was an epic screwup. Getting married on a whim to the woman he spent his life competing with? It felt like some kind of cheesy rom-com setup, except for the fact that this was his actual life. A life that was now entwined with Taylor Cousins. This was not on his life plan. Marriage, sure—down the line, but now? With Taylor Cousins? It was a messy situation, and one that he did not want to get out. He'd worked so hard to be better, to be a worthy man. Someone that people could look up to, and not because of the size of his bank balance or the caliber of his car. He'd never been a person who wanted wealth, or to flash the cash. His Rolex was a present from his grandfather, but he didn't wear it because it was a status symbol. He wore it because his grandfather was a good man, all things considered.

Sebastian had come to Vegas, out of the reach of his family, to make that life. To be happy with who he saw staring back in the mirror every morning. To save lives and rise to the top of his field through hard work and not because of his father's surname, or any of the connections it came with. Those connections were like tentacles, slimy and ever reaching if you didn't keep swimming.

And then one night had derailed everything. The woman who he found equally attractive and annoying had caused him to go off course, and now he was in danger of losing his direction altogether. The residency was vital—so he could stay in Vegas, in his new life. He didn't have time to worry about another person. A person that he couldn't stop picturing naked. The little noises she made when he whispered dirty things against her neck would be the soundtrack in his head for years to come. She was so…sexy. So utterly in sync with his body. He should have known, really. She had already spent every waking moment in his head since he met her, but now those sounds, those images…

He'd had to steel himself to call her. To risk making it worse by hearing her voice on the phone, and then she hadn't even bothered to answer. His wife didn't even want to speak to him. It reminded him of his parents' marriage. The way they spent their time in awkward silence, indifference seeping through their every pore when they were near each other. Wasn't this precisely the reason why he'd never wanted to get married in the first place? With his job, he'd be at work a lot, and that was a marriage killer even for people madly in love. He didn't want to split himself in half like that, when the chances of something real were fleeting at best.

He had too much baggage to date. When you let someone in, they wanted pieces of you. Details about family and what drove them to live the life they did. What was he supposed to say? People always made assumptions about him anyway, no matter what he did. Here in Vegas, he was him. The man he wanted to be, and he wasn't there yet. He needed the next step, and a reckless night stemming from a dare was a threat to everything he'd sacrificed.

The irony of the fact that his nemesis turned reluctant wife was the one person who seemed to see him better than anyone else wasn't lost on him either. Nor the fact that even with all she saw in him, she still rejected his calls, his attempts to put things right. The whole thing was making him tear his hair out.

He needed to get a handle on this, before things got out of control at work too. He needed to get the residency spot and keep his personal life clean. Neither of them could afford any scandals. He knew Taylor would be thinking the same thing, so why wasn't she answering his calls? It wasn't like her to hide from anything. The woman was ferocious.

They needed a game plan, and Patrick laughing at him was the last thing he needed at the minute. Sometimes he despaired at his friend, and his happy-go-lucky outlook on life. Sometimes things were just not easy breezy.

"It's not funny, man. This is serious."

"I bet. You spent the whole night in that hotel

room too. Some wedding night, eh? You know what they say about angry sex."

"I am not discussing that with you," Sebastian growled.

"Right," Patrick smirked, his eyes sparkling with mirth. "No wonder an annulment hasn't been mentioned. Consummated hard, did you?"

Sebastian turned to his friend and said in a low voice, "That's between me and her."

Patrick cleared his throat, looking more than a little sheepish. "Geez. Sorry. I didn't realize it was such a touchy subject."

"My marriage? Yeah, it's a sore spot."

"Well, what does Taylor say? Have you filed to get this sorted out?"

Sebastian huffed out a sigh, checking his phone for the twentieth time that morning. "I haven't spoken to her yet, but I will. I am waiting on my lawyer, but she needs to be part of it. We just need to get it sorted fast." He looked around him at the patients, visitors and colleagues all around him. "Suffice to say, no one can know about this. With the residency spots and everything else, it would be bad for both of us, and definitely bad for you if you go cracking jokes. Don't talk to her about this either, just leave her alone, okay?"

Patrick held up his hands in mock surrender as they paid for their coffees and headed toward the ER to start rounds. As Sebastian let the caffeine inject some energy into his frazzled body, he wondered what Taylor would be like when she clapped eyes on him again. Whether she was feeling as confused by their night together as he was. He'd seen her face when she saw the condom wrappers on the nightstand, the marriage certificate and wedding photo on the table with the ring boxes. He'd been in a state of shock himself that morning, but over the weekend more and more of their time together had come back to haunt him. He had dared her to get married, and she'd gone along with it.

He hadn't been thinking when he said it. It was a throwaway comment he made. They were outside the chapel, and he looked at her and just said it: "I dare you to marry me."

He thought she'd laugh, call him stupid, but she didn't. She glanced at the chapel, and that was it. She agreed, and he should have shut it down. Told her he was joking, backed down. Only that wasn't them, was it? Maybe on some drunken level in his head it had been a test. To see if she would reject him outright. Who knew? He'd need a therapist to sort through that one.

They'd entered the chapel, and that was that. It was happening. One swipe of his card and they were picking the package and walking down the aisle. They'd laughed throughout the whole thing, and when Elvis had told him it was time to kiss the bride, he'd never thought for one minute that it would lead to what it did.

Passion. Hunger. Pure, unadulterated want. As soon as their lips touched, it was game on. Light the touch paper and stand well back. As soon as the marriage certificate was in their hands, they were in the back of a cab making out. They barely made it out of the elevator with their clothes on. Drunk he might have been, but there was no forgetting the way she felt in his arms. The way her body reacted to his touch, and the pure pleasure he felt. They were like…well, newlyweds.

Till the reality had set in, and he was waking up with a wife who was not only in competition with him but hated him intensely. And now he was wondering why it bothered him so much that she wouldn't take his calls.

When the two men walked into the ER department, it was the typical Monday-morning glut of patients that faced them. People who waited till the weekend rush was over to show up with their various injuries and ailments, as well as the usual emergencies and ambulance intakes.

"Jesus," Patrick muttered as they drained their coffee cups and threw them into the nearest bin. "Happy Monday to us."

"Yep, back to reality indeed," Sebastian moaned, scanning the crowd for Taylor's face. "She's not here. Do you see any of the other interns?"

Patrick looked around the busy room. "Nope. Can't see them or your wife. Why don't you call her?"

Sebastian clenched his fists by his sides. Sometimes, he wondered why they were friends in the first place. It was like Patrick didn't listen to a thing that was said. He could feel his frustration tipping over into slight rage.

"I tried to call her, remember? She didn't answer!"

"Whoops. Looks like the honeymoon period is over for you and Cousins already." When Sebastian turned to give him a piece of his mind, he was holding up the photo from their wedding. Which of course Sebastian had sent him when Patrick didn't believe that he was actually telling the truth about their drunken wedding. "Such a shame too. Look, you were both so happy about becoming Mr. and Mrs. Brown!"

What came next happened so fast and so slow all at once. It was as though the universe thought, *I know what will screw Sebastian up in this moment*. It felt like it took an age for Patrick to spot something over Sebastian's shoulder, something that made the blood curdle in his veins and his face drop lower than a snake's belly. He heard the sharp intake of breath that was unmistakably coming from Taylor's lips, and the clearing of a throat that inspired fear in every intern in the hospital.

"Dude," Patrick half whispered, still holding up the phone with the wedding photo displayed for all to see. "I'm sorry."

When Sebastian turned around, Dr. Ashanda was standing there, flanked on each side by shocked-looking interns. Taylor and Selina were both on her left, and the look on Taylor's face made his blood run cold. She looked upset and enraged all at the same time; her cheeks were bright red and Selina was hanging on to her as if she'd drop to the floor without her support. Selina was glaring at Patrick like he was a dog who'd just chewed up her favorite slippers. And done a doo-doo on the carpet to boot.

"Dr. Brown, Dr. Cousins. A moment, please," Dr. Ashanda said, folding her arms across her chest. "In my office. The rest of you, go to the nurses' station and start treating patients. Anything surgical, refer it to your attendings." She looked Patrick up and down. "No phones on my ER floor, Dr. Rowan. You know where to go, right?"

"Patient charts," he pouted. "I know."

"Good luck," Selina called out to them, earning her a sour look from Dr. Ashanda as they followed her meekly to her office.

"Take a seat," she directed as she closed the door behind them. Sebastian turned to Taylor, but she wouldn't meet his eye. This was bad. He had to fix this, for both of them.

"Dr. Ashanda," he said softly. "This isn't what it looks like."

She quirked a dark brow at him, steepling her

fingers as she sat down behind her desk like the formidable figure she was. Framed certificates and awards lined the dark walnut bookshelves behind her, a wall of achievements that both doctors before her coveted for themselves. It couldn't end like this. They had both worked too hard to be derailed by one weekend's choices.

"It isn't? Because, Doctors, it looks to me like two of the best interns I have ever had under my care decided to not only take my advice to have a good weekend to heart but ran with it a little too far. Which is something that I will not tolerate for any future resident. My program is the best in the country for a reason. Because I only pick the best doctors. Surgeons under my tutelage do not make rash mistakes, in surgery or real life.

"So I ask, what is going on? It's no secret that the two of you have an interesting working relationship. I chose to ignore that because in my opinion, competing with each other makes you both better surgeons. A true marriage I could work with, but the circumstances of how it came to be? That makes the difference between becoming a resident here or taking this, whatever it is, to another hospital." Her lips were so pursed now they almost disappeared altogether. "We might be in Vegas, but I can assure you that weddings on a whim are not something I look for when choosing future star surgeons."

"I… We…er…" Taylor stammered.

When Sebastian looked at Taylor, he felt sick. What he saw there was pure fear. A resignation. They couldn't tell the truth now, even if they wanted to.

"So, how long has this been going on?" Dr. Ashanda pressed.

"It isn't going on, Doctor—"

Taylor was going to fess up. He knew it as sure as he knew his own name. She was going to tell the truth, and then both of their dreams would be dead in the water. He thought of his father, how he would have loved this. His son, failing, and taking another fine surgeon with him. *Not going to happen, Pops.* He just hoped that Taylor would pick up on his plan fast enough to play along. Scrambling, he grabbed for something in his pocket and brandished it like Frodo.

"I'm sorry, Dr. Ashanda." He put the ring on his wedding finger and reached for Taylor's hand. She tried to pull back, but he gripped tighter, giving her a pointed look. She stared back, her parted lips slowly closing as they spoke to each other through their gaze. She squeezed his hand, just once, a barely there pressure.

He shot her a tiny nod before turning back to their mentor. "The truth is, Dr. Cousins and I have been in a secret relationship for some time. You're right, we did take the opportunity this weekend to get married, but it wasn't on some whim. We are serious about each other, but our careers are paramount. We knew that if the hospital knew about our status then our residency applications might be in jeopardy, but we are both committed to the Valley, and our work. Given that we could end up in separate states in a few weeks, we decided not to wait any longer."

Dr. Ashanda didn't speak for a moment. The only sound in the room was Taylor's heavy breaths and the tapping of their mentor's foot.

"So all this time, the competition between you two? The back chatting? It's all been part of a romantic relationship?"

"Not exactly," Taylor muttered, squeezing Sebastian's fingers tighter.

"Well, yes and no. Taylor and I—" He felt another death squeeze. He didn't think she was even aware she was doing it, touching him like that. He could feel her emotions swirling right along with his own. "We're very keen to keep our professional and personal lives separate."

"Until Dr. Rowan flashed your wedding photo in the ER."

"Which he shouldn't have in the first place," Taylor muttered at the side of him.

"That was unfortunate, and we will be speaking to him."

"As will I," Dr. Ashanda said coolly. "Well, if you are in fact in a committed relationship, and living together—"

"Living together? I live with Selina!" Taylor protested.

"Yes, honey." Sebastian risked being punched in the face by lifting her hand to his lips and dropping a quick kiss on it. "Dr. Cousins does in fact live with Selina."

Dr. Ashanda clicked her teeth together. "So, you are married but live separately." She leaned forward in her chair. "Highly unusual. I don't know what HR is going to make of this, or the selection committee for the residency program. It's not exactly ideal. Undisclosed relationships are frowned upon, to say the least." She pressed her lips together. "If this really is how you say it is at all."

They were losing her, he could tell. She wasn't buying it, and why would she? Her interns had been at each other's throat for the entirety of their internship years and now they were supposed to be madly in love? He needed to salvage this. He looked to Taylor, and seeing the fear and resignation in her face rise up once again, he pulled the rip cord and jumped. Sitting straight in his chair, he pulled her hand closer in his lap and looked Dr. Ashanda straight in the eyes.

"Dr. Ashanda, we were planning to discuss this with you, and HR. Dr. Cousins is in fact moving in with me this weekend. We wanted to wait till after marriage, you understand. Do things right."

Did her eyebrows just lift? Wow, I didn't think

they moved that way. "I also think that given you were not aware of our very serious relationship till this morning, then this proves that we can maintain our professional boundaries and keep our private life just that. I will of course speak to the other interns if needed, but we both deserve to stay here, Dr. Ashanda. With respect, you said yourself that we are two of the best interns and that isn't going to change. We will continue to challenge each other as we did before, and our marital status will not impact that."

Taylor sat forward in her chair then, and to his surprise, she pulled his arm closer.

"That's right. We both really want to stay at the Valley. More than ever. My family live here, and your department is the best in the country. I for one am not planning to let anything get in my way of that residency."

Sebastian couldn't stop the smile erupting on his face. There she was, the feisty woman he was used to. They could do this, right? Fake a marriage? Hell, his parents did it well enough. Had done for years, and they had liked each other, once upon a time. Or maybe it was always just an arrangement of convenience. The thought that he might be similar to his dad now in that way bothered him, but he pushed that revelation aside to process later.

Dr. Ashanda sat back in her chair, and the pair of them didn't draw breath till she spoke again.

"Fine. Go see HR after rounds, get this on record."

"Of course," Taylor spluttered. "We will do it today."

"Update your new address details while you're at it. I'll speak to Dr. Rowan and the other interns myself, and if there are any issues or questions, they can direct them to myself or HR."

"Thank you," Sebastian said, hoping his voice didn't sound as shaky as he felt. "We just want to work."

"Good." She nodded, dismissing them. They were almost at the door when she called their names. "And congratulations to you both. While I am very surprised at this development, I have to say that it explains a lot. As long as it doesn't affect your work going forward, then I don't see an issue with the residencies either." She actually smiled at them. "I hope you're very happy together in your new adventure."

Sebastian sagged against the door after they thanked her sheepishly and made their escape. Taylor was as white as a sheet, picking her fingers, which was a sure sign she was anxious.

"Well," he sighed. "That went well."

"Went well?" She grabbed his hand again, pulling him down the corridor and dragging him behind her into a supply closet. "Are you fricking kidding me, Brown? What the hell was that?"

"That was me saving our asses, Cousins. The

jig was up. Did you want to admit to the mentor you worship that we got drunk and married on a dare? That we have wedding rings and matching hickies because of some stupid attraction?"

"Attraction? You're...attracted to me?"

Crap. Why did I say that?

"Rivalry. Whatever." He dragged his hands through his hair, feeling the confusing sting of rejection.

She blushed, which made him think of how her cheeks had reddened that night too. When he drove into her till she threw her head back on a throaty moan. *Focus, Seb. Not the time.*

"Look, we were both there that night. I think that we can agree that we fancy each other on a basic level at least. It doesn't mean anything. Neither of us want a relationship."

"Right," she agreed and nodded, her movements slow. "Of course. I just panicked in there. I never wanted this to come out." When her eyes met his again, she almost looked...regretful. "She wouldn't give us the spots if she knew the truth."

"No, of course not. She'd blow us both out of the water for the residencies if she thought we were that reckless. She practically said as much. She hates people bringing their personal lives into work. Remember the screamer?"

She half giggled, and something in his chest loosened at the sound. "Oh yeah. That was bad.

I thought Dr. Ashanda was going to pin him to the surgical board."

"Exactly. The news was already out there about us. I just spun a better light on it. You saw her reaction—she bought it. She thinks we were together all this time, and we proved we still work harder than anyone else. Now we just have to play along, till the residencies get announced at least. We can make a plan, together. Work everything out for when the dust settles. We can still get divorced down the line, but for now, we need to play it right, be the happy couple when people are around. It's the only way we both get what we want out of this, right?"

She was pacing now, which meant that her brain was working overtime. That was just as well, because it bought him a minute too. They'd had to do it; he'd seen the wheels turning in Dr. Ashanda's brilliant mind. The way her body tensed up at the thought of two of her interns disappointing her. If they'd told the truth, their careers would be toast right now. As he watched his new wife pace in front of him, he thought of the implications of all of this. He was tied to this woman now, whether he liked it or not, and the weight of responsibility weighed heavy on him. He had to make this right, for both of them. A scandal was unthinkable. He needed this career, needed to prove himself. He'd finally clawed himself a life he was proud of, and he wasn't going to let it go without a fight.

"So, we're married. We put a pin in the divorce till we get the spots." She was still pacing, but she'd slowed down at least. He knew she was thinking out loud, her way of processing. She did it when she was making treatment plans. When she studied and thought no one was around to hear her talking to herself. "We play our parts as a married couple. As far as everyone knows now, it's real. Like, we're in love."

"I guess so, yeah. And you'll have to move in with me. Just for now. You saw how she reacted when she knew we didn't live together—imagine if we didn't update our addresses like she asked! She'd sniff us out in two seconds. It will make the whole ruse easier for people to believe too. Just for now, I think we have to go with it."

"Well, I gathered that. Who knew that our boss was such a traditionalist, huh?" Her nose wrinkled up, and he willed his own breathing to slow down. "Where do you live again?"

"I have a place near the hospital," he answered. "It's a two-bedroom apartment so we don't have to share a room. But we have to make it look real from now on, I guess. We could take some photos, put them on social media." His socials were all locked as private anyway. He'd made sure of that. His family would never know.

Her snort rang out loud in the enclosed space.

"Yeah, because I would love my family to find out. I've spent years single, Brown. If they find out I got married, they would definitely know something was off. Besides, the photo is kind of why we're here in the first place. Why did you send it to Patrick?"

"I wasn't thinking about him showing it to anyone. I needed to talk to someone, you know? He didn't believe me till I showed him the proof. And for the record, I am going to murder him the first chance I get."

She laughed. An honest-to-god laugh. "Yeah, well, judging by Selina's face, he might already be stuffed into a medical waste bin by now. He's such an idiot." She bit at her lip. "Does he know… everything about that night?"

Whoops. Now it was his turn to blush. Hard. "Well, he doesn't know details, but he knows we can't annul. Does Selina know?"

There she went again with the lip biting. *Did she always do that? Why am I noticing it now?* She wasn't looking him in the eye either. *Did she tell Selina about the steamy part of our night?* Damn it. Now he wanted to know what she'd said. What she remembered, how it made her feel. *No. No, no, no. I really don't want to know. Nothing good can come from that.*

"Er…yeah. Bits." *Bits? Which bits? Good or bad? I have to know.*

"Oh yeah? What did you tell her?"

She cleared her throat, picked at her fingers. "Nothing much, but she knows that we had to get divorced."

Riiggghhtt. As usual, she wasn't going to give anything away. He could read her like a book, but he needed actual words this time. When he didn't get them, his annoyance grew. This woman had irked him and intrigued him from the first day they'd met. It looked like that wasn't about to change, and worse still, now he remembered how she sounded in bed. How she felt. This was precisely why relationships were out of bounds for him. He didn't want to let another person get close. To know the real him and find him lacking. His family were always telling him growing up that he didn't pass muster. Because he had his own mind, his own opinions. Wanted to make his own way. He was sick of feeling like a disappointment, less than. Letting Taylor get so close had sneaked up on him, and now they were stuck—fighting each other and not able to do anything but pretend to be something neither of them remotely wanted.

"Yeah. I checked with my lawyer," he said, pulling himself out of thoughts he definitely shouldn't be having. "And it turns out a divorce will take some time, which you would know if you'd answered your phone this weekend. We could have made a better plan if we'd talked. Maybe we could have gone to HR first, got out ahead of this before Patrick had the chance to out us like he did."

She didn't meet his eye yet again. Since the wedding night, she'd shied away from her usual glares and stares. *Another part of our new dynamic, it seems.*

"Yeah, well, we didn't. I needed a minute to process everything." Her shoulders deflated in front of him, which made her look even smaller to his imposing size. "I can't believe this is happening. I really have to live with you? Pretend that we like each other? What about kissing?" She looked mortified, which did sting a little, but she had a point. It's not like they had done that sober. He hadn't exactly been planning to suck face with her either. It was bad enough having the carnal knowledge he already had of her zinging through his brain. "Oh god, I don't even know about your family. Shouldn't a wife know that kind of stuff?"

Sebstiana balked at the question. She didn't need to know them—*he* didn't. Walking away from them also meant he didn't owe them a detail of his future, and that included his fake wife.

"We're not close, and I'm not exactly planning on telling them about all this. If anyone asks you questions at work, just tell them it's our private business. If this were real, we wouldn't be canoodling on the corridors, would we?"

She raised a brow, her lips quirking into a wry grin. "Canoodling? How old are you, seventy?"

"Yep." He shuffled her toward the door. "Come on, we need to face this. I'll text you my address, or I can give you a ride if you wait for me tonight. Might as well start as we mean to go on if we're going to pull this off."

"Ride together?"

Sebastian sighed theatrically. "We've bumped uglies, wifey. We can survive a car ride without killing each other, and you don't have a car, remember?"

"Oh." There it was again, that cute little blush of hers. He was starting to get a taste for it. For making it happen. He needed to watch that; it was a habit he couldn't afford. This whole thing was distracting enough as it was, without his nether regions chiming in. "And also, eww." *Well, that'll work.* She definitely wasn't feeling the same. She was back to being the same stubborn woman he loved to bait.

"Cousins..." He could almost see the back of his own head with the epic eye roll he shot her. "We agreed to do this. It's a lift, not a golden wedding anniversary."

"Okay, fine. I'll have to speak to Selina though. I can't pay rent for two places. I have...obligations."

"So don't," he told her, his need to make this right surging forward. He'd seen how frugal she was, bringing her own lunch to work. Using public transport even though he knew she could drive. He wasn't rich by his family's measure of wealth, but he was comfortable. If she was his real wife, he would look after her. For appearances' sake, it made sense. "My place is paid for; I manage on my own. You can keep paying Selina your share if she needs it, till we sort this out."

"That's another point," she said, stilling in front of the door. "How long are we supposed to keep this going for? Till our silver anniversary? Till the kids come of age?"

"Kids?"

"Well, I don't know! I've never been in this situation before."

"Oh. Sure, because I have a bunch of fake wives hidden in my closet."

"Shut up, Brown! This isn't going to work! They're never going to buy that we like each other, let alone that we love each other enough to get married in secret! It's all going to go wrong, and then it's going to get so much worse, and we're going to lose everything! We can't pull this off, we just can't." She was spiraling, too far in her head, and her voice was just about breaking the sound barrier. "I've got to go. Don't follow me right out—give it a few minutes." Visibly rattled, she ran a hand down her hair, her clothes, and with a bone-shuddering sigh of frustration, she left him standing there in the closet.

CHAPTER FIVE

MY WIFE HATES ME, and I can't say I blame her either.

Stupid. Reckless. That was the theme of the Vegas night they had got hitched, but now they had to live with the consequences together. Taylor, of all people, was now hitched to this wagon and all Sebastian wanted to do was throw her off it, because sooner or later, the wonky wheels were going to fall off and crush them both under its weight. She'd kept her distance during rounds, and the other interns were too scared to say anything in front of Dr. Ashanda. Patrick was nowhere to be seen, probably running some ghastly errand as punishment.

Good, he thought petulantly.

The ER was thankfully busy, so he lost himself in work for a while. Kept on task and pretended not to notice the odd stares and whispers from the nurses and other staff he crossed paths with. HR had obviously been briefed by Dr. Ashanda, because when he'd gone to see them to log their relationship and new marital status, they barely batted an eyelid.

It wasn't that relationships were banned. After all, medical personnel worked long hours and often didn't see a lot of life outside the hospital. Working in close proximity with each other often made relationships, but it broke them too; hence the necessity of logging things with HR. Managing staff was hard enough without the added stress of relationship breakdowns leading to harassment claims and the like.

His new marriage was a prime example, given that they had both been very vocal about their dislike for each other. Their respective and often clashing competitive streaks had often been brought up around the hospital. People knew that when they were bickering it was best to stay out of the way. Which Sebastian could relate to right now, when his wife walked around the corner, saw him and abruptly turned tail.

He ran to catch up with her, his gut gnawing. He didn't like this new dynamic of theirs; it was too weird. Running away was not Taylor's style. She wasn't usually pleased to see him of course, but actively avoiding him without even a barb bothered him. It was their thing, to wind each other up. It made his day better, crossing paths with her and sharing a bit of cutting banter. He'd found her attractive, sure—but before their night on the strip he'd never planned to act on it.

He'd never been interested in anyone at the hospital. He didn't see the point of marriage. Of letting someone else in, having to explain his past and how it affected his decisions in life. He was doing fine without a partner, happy enough with his work. The intern currently running from him though? She was in his head now, in more ways than one. Some of those ways were pretty dirty too, if memory served.

"Not so fast, wifey." He tried a jovial tone, but her look told him he'd missed the mark. Scowling at someone while arching a brow was a strategic skill to possess, but his new spouse had managed to master it. "Good day?"

"Don't call me that," she hissed. "And it's not a good day, for the record. Not when people are openly gossiping about the current state of my uterus! Our sex life is the topic of the day!"

Huh? Oh god. Not now. Our sex life. It made him think of them together. Her, in the Vegas hotel room, legs wrapped around him. Pinned to the door, she'd gasped as he entered her, hard and slow. The sex flashbacks needed to stop. They were starting to bother him, in more ways than one.

"So deep," she'd mumbled, before saying something else he'd missed in his fever to capture her kissable lips. Lips he couldn't help but study again. They were pursed now though, moving rapidly.

"Brown? Are you even listening to me?"

"Huh?" Balking as he came to, he took in her hunched shoulders and tapping foot. "Sorry, yeah. Something about a uterus?"

She practically growled as she grasped the lapels of his white coat and yanked him toward the door to the storage closet again.

We have to stop meeting like this, he thought childishly. This communicating-in-a-closet thing was starting to become a part of their new strange life together. The second they were behind the closed door, she let go. Which was just as well, because being together behind a door like this, with her panting breaths and searching eyes, was doing nothing to quell his sudden urge to reenact the memory that had just slammed through him.

It was starting to become a problem. He'd always thought she was cute. Beautiful, even, but like a work of art in the Louvre. You didn't touch the *Mona Lisa*, did you? Nope. Because it wasn't yours to touch, would never be. So you just stared at it, appreciated it for how perfect it was, and moved along. Now he felt like the security guard assigned to the painting. He still couldn't touch it, but it was there, every time he went to work. Only now he would have the damn thing in his house too.

"Are you malfunctioning or something?" she demanded.

Yep, she was still mad, and glaring at him,

oblivious to the horny thoughts he was trying to push out of his head. He needed to get a grip on himself. That night was the start of all this, and going for round two was definitely not happening, nor was it a good idea.

"My uterus is the problem here, and apparently the hot topic of question time among the staff. I overheard them at the nurses' station, saying I was probably knocked up!"

"You're… Oh…people think you're pregnant? They think that's the reason we got married?"

"Yep. People are not buying this as some kind of love match, and why would they? It's pretty obvious we don't like each other. After Vegas, anyone with half a brain would ask what they are thinking. With Patrick outing us like that, and then being summoned to Dr. Ashanda's office, it's not a good look."

She had a point. They had been pretty obvious with their natural rivalry. Wouldn't he wonder the same thing, if it happened between two of his colleagues? She was wringing her hands again. Rubbing them together as if she was trying to ground herself.

You did this, a voice rang inside his head, sounding suspiciously like his father's. *You messed up, and now everyone around you has to face the consequences.* Well, screw him. Sebastian had walked away from his family for a reason, away from their expectations, their greed and their indifference to their son, and right now Taylor was as close to a family as it got. Even if it was fake, he still had a responsibility to her. They'd started this thing together, and they needed to see it through as a couple too.

"Leave it with me. We stick to the plan. You move in, tonight. We don't answer questions. It's not anyone's business but ours. This is a hospital, not a coffee shop. Dr. Ashanda hates gossip—she'll shut it down on her end if she hears about it. Fingers crossed it won't come to that, if we stick to the plan. I've got you, Cousins. Just for once, trust me."

Her eyes narrowed, and he could feel the defeat and skepticism rolling off her. It bothered him more than he ever thought it would. He wanted to make it right somehow. Taylor might only be his wife on paper, but they were together in this. Partners in this death-do-us-part subterfuge.

"Wh-why?" she stammered after a pause that made his guts wrench. "What are you going to do?"

"Just let me handle it, okay? End of shift. Give me till then." A commotion beyond the doors had them both turning their heads. "Trust me?"

She looked him in the eyes, and for a second they just took each other in. "Okay." She nodded. "End of shift."

They could hear shouting erupt from outside, and the pair of them dashed back to work.

CHAPTER SIX

"YOU'VE GOT TO be kidding me."

Taylor had seen many sights in this crazy corner of the world, but this had to be up there.

"I hate you, Gus! I never should have married you!"

The bride being wheeled through the emergency room doors looked like Carrie à la Stephen King, but she was obviously not feeling whatever injuries she'd sustained. Nope. She was too busy trying to claw at the guy being wheeled in alongside her, and he was shouting right back.

"Oh yeah? Well, tough, Hannah! Because we just did it, so you're stuck with me! I can't believe you're blaming me for this either! I wasn't protesting!"

"Protesting?" Taylor asked aloud, and the two of them turned to look at her as she headed over. The EMTs were looking decidedly unamused at their antics, and very happy to see her. "This is from a protest?"

"Yep. There's an abortion clinic right by the

Little Chapel. These guys had just come out of the chapel and got caught in the wrong place at the wrong time." The EMT nodded to the bride, who was still chewing out her very sad looking groom. "It's fake blood, but she's got a fractured ankle from taking a dip off the sidewalk. She was stepped on during the melee, bruising on her torso and stomach. She didn't lose consciousness when she hit the floor, but there is the possibility of glass shards in her wound. With the fake blood and the movement when transporting we didn't want to dislodge anything."

"Okay, and the groom?"

"Augustus Pettigrew, twenty-nine, goes by Gus. He has a head laceration from tackling one of the guys. Superficial scratches and shallow cuts from some broken glass. He crawled along the floor to get to his wife, through the debris."

"Aw," a passing nurse trilled. "That's pretty romantic, especially on a wedding day!"

"Sure," the EMT huffed. "I'll tell that to dispatch when I inform them that they're a crew down while we wash a bunch of fake blood off our rig. I bet the romance will soften the blow." He quirked a sarcastic brow at the nurse, who stuck her tongue out in response.

"Okay, well, we can take it from here," Taylor cut in, eager to get Mr. Chirpy back to his rig and her back to sorting out her new intake. "Thanks, and sorry about your rig."

He harrumphed something barely audible and shuffled off with his equally miserable looking colleague.

"Everything okay?" And of course, just to top her day off, here her husband came to save the damn day.

"Well, the ER is slammed, the EMTs are fed up and we have a bride covered in fake blood who is currently arguing with her new hubby, so yeah!" She turned to give him a sarcastic thumbs-up. "Great!"

Sebastian narrowed his eyes but didn't bother to respond. Which was weird, because right about now he would usually say something cutting back. Was he mad that she didn't say she trusted him? Nah. That couldn't be it. He was probably just feeling as weird as she was about facing their colleagues in light of everything. She still felt angry about the whole thing, and people thinking she was carrying his child wasn't helping her mood toward him either.

"Okay, I'll take the groom, you take the bride." When she did nothing but glower in reply, he sighed heavily. "Look, we have to nail this ER rotation—and work together, right?" He leaned in close, his hand running down the length of her arm from shoulder to wrist. She could feel every little movement through her clothing and resisted the reaction she felt deep down in her gut. "Plus, dear wifey, we are supposed to be madly in love and not just together for the sake of a fictional baby. I said I would take care of this, but you have to play your part as my adoring spouse." His lips brushed against her ear, and this time nothing could stop the resulting shudder that erupted through her.

This would be so much easier if he was ugly. Far more endurable if I didn't know what he looked and felt like naked too. Snap out of it, Taylor.

"Fine," she agreed. "Let's get them separated though, before the ER turns into a boxing ring."

"Deal." He flashed her a cheeky smile, one that a couple of the nurses simpered over. "Gus, some wedding day, huh?"

Taylor ignored the stares from the staff around her and turned her attention to the bride.

"Hi, I'm Dr. Cousins, one of the surgical interns here."

"Intern? Isn't that like a trainee or something?"

"I am a doctor. I am still training for the surgical aspect, but I can assure you that I can treat you, and if there is anything surgical that's needed it will be overseen by one of my superiors." She scanned her medical notes on the tablet she was holding. "Shall I call you Hannah, or Mrs. Pettigrew?"

"Hannah's fine," she retorted glumly. "I'm not sure I want to be a Pettigrew after today. Ouch!"

Taylor winced. "Sorry, I am trying to be gentle." She motioned for one of the nurses to come over. "Hannah here will need an X-ray, and if you could let orthopedics know we need a consult."

She turned back to her patient, who was now softly crying. "I'm sorry, I know that you're in some distress but we can't give you any more pain relief just yet." She looked at the ruined wedding dress, realizing that she was going to have to change into a gown. "We can get you changed into something more comfortable for now, but we will need to do an ultrasound to check on your abdominal injuries. Do you have pain anywhere else?"

"Just my heart. I thought today was going to be perfect, you know?" She toyed with a piece of her dress, torn and tattered at her thigh. "We don't have a lot of money. Gus said that we didn't need a lot, and we live close. It made sense, but now look! We barely got outside and then they all just jumped on us! We weren't even in the clinic! They were all shouting, and Gus tried to get me out of there but then they threw blood!"

"It's not actually blood—"

Hannah's narrowed eyes cut to hers. "I know it's not actual blood, but I thought it was and this dress is rented! Look at it! I'll never get my deposit back now!"

Taylor watched the new bride dissolve into tears and felt her heart break for her. They were actually in love. Their wedding was supposed to be something special, not ending up in the ER at each other's throats. In the next cubicle, she could hear Sebastian comforting the groom as he tended to his lacerations. She could do this. She could pretend. Hell, she would have to be nicer to him, but she could do that too. For this job, for her future, and the women who raised her.

"Don't worry about the deposit," she said, her voice softer now. "All that matters is that you are both okay, and have each other, right? Don't let your day be ruined by other people."

When the nurse came in, the two women helped her pull off the dress and get into a gown. Her stomach was showing signs of bruising already. Poor woman. This could have been far worse. Someone could have been killed, and for what? A misunderstanding?

She readied the jelly, squirting it onto Hannah's stomach and moving the wand over her skin as gently as she could.

"Am I okay?" Hannah asked, her tears dry now. "This is supposed to be my wedding night. I really don't want to be in here instead."

Taylor gave her a warm smile, turning back to the screen. "Everything looks healthy. No signs of internal bleeding, and…" Her voice gave out as she saw the image on the screen. Moving over it, she checked every detail. "Er… Hannah, would you like to move to another booth? I have some important information for you." She tilted her head toward the curtain, behind which Gus was still grumbling in pain and telling Sebastian what he would like to do to the protesters for hurting his wife. "In private."

Hannah's eyes narrowed, and she looked at the screen, which was tilted away from her gaze. "No, I… Just tell me."

Taylor turned the screen toward Hannah, pointing to a little bean-shape image. "You're pregnant, Hannah. About three months along, I believe. We will take measurements to give you an exact date, but—"

"I'm pregnant…" Hannah murmured, looking at the screen in awe. "Really?"

Taylor matched her grin. "Yes, and the baby is perfectly healthy. I would like to keep you in for observation, and you will need to stay off your ankle but—"

Hannah grabbed for the curtain separating them, and Taylor helped to pull it back.

"Gus!"

Gus, who was wincing as Sebastian pulled another shard of glass out of his bloody forearm, whipped his head to his wife. "Hannah! You okay?"

"Yeah," she blubbered. "I'm pregnant!"

Gus shot up on his gurney, Sebastian just managing to move his surgical tweezers out of the way in time. "Hey!" He pushed him back down.

"Congratulations, man, but please, stay still till I finish patching you up."

If Gus heard him, he made no acknowledgment. His whole face was lit up with pure joy. "Really?" His brows knitted together. "Is the baby okay? You got hurt."

"I'm fine." She looked down at her belly, as Taylor wiped the jelly off and covered it with the gown. "Right, Doctor?" She flashed a look of panic Taylor's way. "I am going to be okay, right?"

"We might just need to adjust your treatment plan for that ankle, but yes, you're good. I'll call OB and they can give you a full workup."

"Stupid protesters," Gus fumed. "Ironic that they almost killed a baby protesting abortion! I'm so sorry, honey. I should have protected you."

The pair of them reached out for the other, linking their fingers across the space. "You did protect me, honey. You got cut up doing it."

The nursing staff around them were all simpering at the pair, and Taylor couldn't help but look Sebastian's way.

"Wow." Collette, one of the nurses who constantly flirted with Sebastian, touched his arm. He shrugged her off. "Must be something in the water, huh? All these surprise babies and marriages."

Taylor felt her jaw tighten, the flush of shame envelop her as the whole room stared at her stomach. Well, not everyone. Hannah and Gus didn't even realize that anyone else was in the hospital, let alone the ER. They were in their very own little love bubble.

How am I in this situation? I want to be known for my skills, not my fictitious personal life.

"Actually, I—" Taylor began.

Sebastian came to stand next to her, snapping off his gloves with an angry flourish.

"My wife and I are here to work, Collette. Not to listen to gossip or discuss our private lives in front of patients." He pulled Taylor closer, his hand tight on her hip. "I'm sure if you have any questions, HR or Dr. Ashanda would be happy to answer them. As for Taylor and I, we are very happy together, and there is no baby." He turned her to him, looking down at her as though she was the most precious thing in the universe. "I want my beautiful, clever bride all to myself for a while, before we start our family."

Jesus, he's a good actor. I almost believe him. Looking up into his huge brown eyes, she wondered what was going on in that head of his. Was he feeling this too, this pull between them? Being this close to him was becoming confusing. Right now, she didn't know whether to slap him or kiss him, and it had never been like this before. His eyes were searching hers, as if he was trying to find some answer out for himself. She cleared her throat, gently pushing at his chest till he released her. She turned to Collette and the others and noticed that Dr. Ashanda was watching from the other side of the room.

"Now," she said and smiled, stepping away from Sebastian so she could draw breath. "Back to work."

The staff all shuffled off, and the room picked up its usual tempo. Sebastian came to stand in front of her as she went to tend to Hannah.

"See?" he told her, his face smug. And…was that a flush to his cheeks? *Nah.* It was probably embarrassment. "Told you I would handle this. I'll see you after work. Parking lot."

When she returned to Hannah, the bride was already smiling at her.

"Damn," she said, rubbing her belly with both hands. "It's definitely a day for lovers, huh? Your husband is nearly as hot as mine."

Taylor's eyes found Sebastian again, as he finished bandaging Gus.

"Almost," she mumbled, before tearing her eyes from him. "Now, let's get that ankle sorted so you can enjoy the rest of your day, huh?"

CHAPTER SEVEN

"Hey! Can I get some help here or not? I've been waiting for hours!"

Taylor headed back over to the man who had been making the ER department a tense environment from the second he'd walked in. After a very weird first night at Sebastian's house, and a night of fitful sleep in a strange bed, she had been hoping that work was going to be the distraction she needed.

Dr. Ashanda had been operating on a double bypass patient all morning, but she'd picked Sebastian to assist her this time. Which was normal—she usually didn't take the two of them at the same time—but it still stung like it always did when he got into the OR and she didn't. She could picture him now, gowned and gloved, working on that precious heart while she tended to the patients who had been flowing through the doors with a variety of ailments.

So far this morning she'd treated a woman who'd had an asthma attack at a smoky BBQ, a workman who'd managed to slice his pinkie finger off with a circular saw and a plethora of food-poisoning patients who'd all eaten some bad shrimp. She'd seen enough bodily fluids to keep her going for the rest of the week, and this guy didn't even seem to be ill. He was agitated though, and he'd already made one of the nurses run off crying with his insults.

"Mr. Prady, as I explained earlier, we are very busy today. You are on the triage list, but we have to work in order of priority. If you could just take a seat, I will try to get to you as soon as possible."

"Bull," he spit. "I'm in pain, and I need attention. Now."

His fists were clenched tight to his sides, his skin pale and sweaty. He kept scratching at his arms, which were filled with angry-looking marks. *Addict.* She'd seen the signs before, had dealt with many patients like this in the past. They got hooked on drugs, prescription or otherwise, and their whole body jonesed for more. Sometimes they ended up in here after an overdose, or a dose of bad street drugs. It was sad, but something about his man set her nerves on edge. People who were this agitated and desperate tended to forget the rules of society, or care.

"Are you listening to me? What kind of doctor are you, anyway? Some kind of newbie? Get me a supervisor already! I need pain relief, now!"

He clutched his side, the opposite side to the one he'd come in holding.

"Okay, sir." She needed to keep him calm. The ER was full of sick or injured people, some of whom were already looking their way with wary expressions. "Take a seat, and I will check your patient file and get you sorted."

He glared at her for a long moment but then gave an acknowledging grunt.

"Two minutes, and then I come looking for you."

Taylor shot him a smile she didn't feel and waited for him to take a seat before heading over to the main desk. Austin, one of the ER nurses, came over and tapped a few keys on the screen.

"Here's his file," he said with a knowing nod.

"Okay, thanks," she said, keeping the easy smile on her face. "Is it what I think it is?"

Austin nodded, showing her the history of Mr. Prady's recent intakes. "He's been to every ER in the city the last few weeks. He's been blacklisted from two of them."

Taylor scanned the file. Mr. Prady was a former construction worker. His file was full of operations from a broken back he suffered years ago on the job. "Poor guy," she murmured. "He's addicted to pain medication. We need to deal with this sensitively, but call security. Get them down here, but inform them of the situation."

"We can't prescribe him anything though,

right? He is healed from his injuries. The pain clinic discharged him months ago."

Taylor pressed her lips together tightly. "No, we can't. We can offer him rehab, but it looks like he's refused every other attempt. We need to tread carefully here. I'll put him in treatment room two. He doesn't need an audience for this and you go tell security where he is."

"Done." Austin nodded. "Just wait for me to get back, okay?"

"Oh, don't worry, I will." She did not want to be alone in a room with him. She could see him getting more and more wound up the more time she spent not dealing with him. She just needed to wait till—

"Will you stop that stupid whining already?"

She heard his booming voice, and her blood went cold. A mother was holding her little boy, who was crying because of a fever. They were waiting on the next available doctor, which would only annoy Mr. Prady more.

"Shut him up! I can't think straight!"

When his fist hit the wall, Taylor didn't wait. She strode right over to him and blocked his view of the terrified boy. Her father used to shout at her like that when he was drunk. She wasn't about to stand by and watch it happen when she could do something. Her mother never stood by either, and she was her mother's daughter through and through.

"Mr. Prady! Please calm down and follow me. We have a treatment room all set up for you."

"Oh yeah?" His unkempt hair fell in front of his glassy eyes, and his hands shook as he pushed it back. "What were you doing over there, huh? Calling security? Looking me up on your little computer!" He was yelling now, spittle forming at the corners of his dry mouth. "It's people like you that did this to me!"

She put her hands out to placate him, to try to calm him down, but he was beyond angry. When he saw her hands outstretched, he lunged. Pain shot up her arms as he squeezed, gripping her tight. Taylor tried to push him backto release herself, but he was far too strong, too angry. The whole ER erupted into chaos, nurses pulling patients out of the way. The little boy was screaming now as his mother grabbed him and ran.

"Security!" she shouted, looking around for Austin, for anyone to give her a hand.

"You stupid stuck-up woman! You don't care about people like me, in pain, struggling! You wanna see how it feels, huh?" His face was pure venom, his skin shiny with sweat as he shook her around like a rag doll.

"Get your hands off my wife!" A booming voice broke through the noise and then Sebastian was there. Wrestling the man's grip away from her with a fury that she'd never seen before.

She hit the deck, her head thudding on the hard

floor. *Ouch.* All she saw for a moment was stars. All she could hear was screaming and shouting. The grunts of men and the squeaking of shoes.

"Taylor," a voice said, and when she opened her eyes, Sebastian was there. "Taylor! You okay?"

Lying on the floor, she assessed her injuries. Tilted her head to the side in time to see security haul off her patient. She tried to get up, but a strong arm pushed her back down.

"Not a chance, Supergirl. You need to get checked out first."

Sebastian's face loomed close, and then she was off the floor and being carried down the corridor.

"Brown, put me down!" She tried to wriggle, but the pain in her head flashed so she ended up clinging to him tighter.

"Careful, and it's Sebastian to you, wifey. What the hell were you doing anyway, taking him on like that?" He headed into the elevator, shooting a look at an orderly, who dipped his head and left them alone. He didn't put her down to press the elevator button either. "You got hurt putting yourself in danger like that," he added as the doors closed.

"I'm fine," she argued, but winced. Every word made her head hurt. She'd well and truly rung her bell hitting the floor like that. "We're alone now. No need for the concerned-husband bit."

"It's not a bit," he snapped back. "You got hurt.

I'm not a monster, Taylor. That guy was trying to take your head off. What did you want me to do, just stand there?" He huffed out a breath, his grip tightening on her. "You're impossible, you know that?"

She'd done it again. He'd done a nice thing and she'd snapped at him. He'd taken on that guy and come to help. It was so hard, this flip-flopping they were doing. She was getting whiplash from the mood swings he evoked.

"I know."

His head snapped down to hers.

"What?"

"I know. I'm sorry. What I should have said is thank you for coming to help. I guess I just feel so weird around you now. I don't know how to act, especially at work."

His scowl softened. "I get it, but we are in this together for however long it takes. Believe it or not, that actually means something to me. You're trying to protect my career too." His jaw clenched. *He was...upset?* "When I saw that guy hurting you, I just reacted. I saw red, okay? I don't want you getting hurt like that. I don't have a lot of family, actually *any* family to speak of. I just—"

Ping. The elevator opened onto the neuro floor, and she heard him curse under his breath. He carried her onto the nearest spare bed, gently settling her on top of the covers. "I'll go get someone; get you checked over. You might have a concussion. I'll tell Dr. Ashanda you'll be out for the day."

"Sebastian, wait."

He was already leaving, and he didn't stop. "I'll work late to pick up the slack; I have tomorrow off anyway. Don't wait up, and don't leave here till you're all checked out. No more heroics, Cousins."

He left without a backward glance, his back ramrod straight.

After speaking to the staff on the neuro floor, Sebastian stomped back to the ER to deal with the aftermath of Mr. Prady. He'd be in the hands of the police now, and security would no doubt want to press charges on behalf of the hospital. Assaulting a member of medical staff was taken seriously. With a bit of luck, this might also be the push he needed to finally get help for his addiction too. Another casualty of the health care system.

Sebastian had seen it many times, and his father was partly to blame. His pharma companies were all about the money. Their view was that if a patient was spending money, it didn't matter whether it was the right thing. It didn't matter whether the pain medication could be managed better or monitored more. It was one of the reasons he'd left in the first place, not wanting to be a cog in their empire.

Sometimes he thought that the only reason his parents had even had a kid was so their legacy would last beyond them, that the Harrison name would live on. Which was partly why he'd changed his surname from Harrison to Brown. His parents didn't care about the little people; they never understood how their greed changed lives. Like the man who'd just attacked Sebastian's fake wife.

His fists clenched involuntarily at the memory of seeing her like that, pinned against the wall. What he'd said to her wasn't a lie. It had been pure adrenaline and instinct, roaring over there to save her. Very alpha, as Selina would say. Even in the hospital setting, he'd had to restrain himself not to pop the guy in the jaw, and he wasn't that man. Addiction had a lot to answer for, and pharma was right at the top of the blame list. He'd seen Mr. Prady here before, a while ago, but it was a very different man who'd hurt his wife today.

She'd been snarky to him, as usual. It was nothing new—it was their thing—but today? He'd hated it. Despised that she'd been like that with him, because he really had just acted out of instinct. While he was grappling with the guy, trying to help security, he'd seen her hit the floor. His whole gut had wrenched. The lines between them were blurring, and he didn't know what to do about it. He didn't want another person to worry about, a distraction from his goal. He couldn't escape it either, thanks to their marital status and the charade they were trying to pull off.

Since walking out on his family, work had been the one sure thing in his life. With his inheritance from his grandfather safely out of his father's grasp, he was comfortable. It had enabled him to follow his dream without racking up debts and living on ramen, but he was alone in his place once the doors were locked. Now he had Taylor there. After last night, with her in his home, and seeing her get hurt today, he was feeling more and more like husband material. And boy, was it chafing.

Dr. Ashanda was all control when he got back to the ER. The little boy and his mom were being treated, and the board was in order with patients steadily being called up for medical assistance.

"Is Dr. Cousins okay?" she asked him the second she saw him.

"Bruising on her upper arms, possible concussion. I took her to neuro for a scan. I don't think she'll be back today, but I'll pick up her work."

He waited for her to say something cutting, moan about losing an intern, but she surprised him.

"Brave wife you have there," she told him with a look of begrudging admiration on her face. "I must admit, I rather thought that it would be the pair of you that ended up in fisticuffs, but you were both willing to go to bat for each other today, and for your patients."

"Er…yeah. Of course. Thank you, Dr. Ashanda. I'm sorry if I overstepped."

She waved him off. "I won't have patients hurting my interns." She looked down her glasses at him. "And I wouldn't expect a husband in love to act any differently. You can start with bed two."

Glad to be dismissed, he scuttled off, ignoring the admiring looks that every nurse in the place was giving him. It seemed like they'd convinced everyone that this marriage of theirs was the real deal. He just needed to remind himself that it was anything but.

CHAPTER EIGHT

SEBASTIAN'S APARTMENT WAS dimly lit and silent when Taylor finally got in from her shift the next night. Locking up behind her, she pulled off her boots with a wince and rolled her ankles to try to ease the tension in her tired limbs. Having avoided a concussion and being given the all-clear, she'd gone back to work with gusto. Especially since she was avoiding Sebastian just as much as he was her. Last night she'd been asleep by the time he'd come home, and she'd sneaked out extra early for rounds. It had been a long, exhausting shift and all she wanted to do was have a shower, eat her body weight in pasta and slump into bed for a solid eight hours.

Padding down the hallway, she saw the lounge light on.

"Sebastian?"

No answer. He was probably out, having a life on his day off. She went to turn off the light that was on in there and stopped in her tracks. He was asleep, laid out on the couch. A textbook was open across his lap, a notepad and pen on the coffee table beside him. A few other books were strewn across the carpet; an empty pizza box open next to them. Judging from the coffee cups and energy drink cans, he'd been there all day.

"Such a nerd," she muttered under her breath as she padded across the carpet on stockinged feet. She started to reach for the lamp switch, but the closer she got to him, the more she took in. She couldn't help herself, watching him sleep. He looked so comfy, so utterly unlike he was at work. At the hospital, he was always in motion. Forever watching, and moving, mobilizing. Even when he was writing up hospital records, his foot was tapping under his desk or his pen was clicking in those long fingers of his. Now he was still. At rest. His chest slowly moving with every slumbering breath. She started to collect the scattered books, resting on her knees to stack them in a pile, when she noticed the hand laid across his chest. The wedding ring glinted on his finger in the lamplight, and she couldn't stop staring at it.

He was wearing his ring, out of work? She only wore hers when she was at the hospital or pinned to her scrub top when she was in surgery, like the other married surgeons had taught her. It was strange, seeing it on his finger, in his place. *Our place now, I guess.*

For the millionth time, she marveled at the turn of events. She was living with her husband. Such a simple sentence but it felt so alien. Even moving in here had been done with little fanfare or fuss. He just welcomed her in after their shift, helped her with her bags. Showed her around. Gave her a key like he was almost happy for her to be there. The odd thing was, it wasn't horrible. His place was actually nice. Neat and big enough for the two of them to rattle around together well enough. Not half as flashy as she'd imagined, which made her feel a lot better about being there.

She looked at his ring again, and down at hers, which was still on her finger after shift. Biting her lip, she was just wondering whether to leave it on when Sebastian woke up.

"What are you looking at?" he suddenly said, cutting through the silence like a sword.

She stumbled back and would have hit the coffee table if he hadn't reached for her. His hands steadied her. "Hey, easy there!"

"You scared the heck out of me!"

Chuckling, he sat up, patting the free couch cushion next to him. "Sorry. You really need to be more careful, you know. That head of yours is going to crack like an egg one of these days."

"Funny," she scoffed before suppressing a yawn. "Almost as funny as when neuro told me my husband was some kind of Adonis, carrying me from danger and checking up on my head."

He rolled his shoulders, chuckling. "Well, thanks to Mr. Prady, our little love story is solid. Had to keep up appearances." He tilted his head, those brown eyes of his roving over her features. "No headaches or anything? How're the arms?"

"Sore." She rubbed at them gingerly. "Purple. My head's fine, no damage."

"None that wasn't there already anyway."

She barely held in her laughter. It was pretty funny, for one of his comebacks.

"I'd say something pithy back, but I'm so tired I don't think my body could take it. Work was crazy today in the ER and Dr. Ashanda had me assisting on a pacemaker placement too. Which was great, but also backbreaking."

"Hard relate. She once had me holding a retractor for six hours straight, I thought my spine was going to snap. Sit down a minute, I'll clean up." He ran his hand through his bed-head hair, which only served to stick it up into tufts. "I didn't mean to fall asleep."

She sat down next to him, sighing when her tired body touched the comfy furniture. "Well, I don't blame you. I could sleep for a week right now."

"Have you eaten anything? I stocked the fridge." He lifted the pizza box, wrinkling his nose. "There's pizza too, if you don't mind reheated grease."

"Nah, I'm good. I just want to shower and rest. Did you spend the whole day studying? What a loser."

He snorted, tidying up the living space around her. "Gee thanks, wifey. I went to the market too, for the food. What do you do on your days off, skydiving?"

"Yep," she smirked. "When I'm not on the pole at the Spearmint Lounge."

"Pole dancing?" He almost dropped the books he was stacking on the table. "Judging from the dancing I've witnessed, I doubt it."

"Hey! Don't insult me, I'm too tired to fight back."

They were still laughing when their eyes met, and the tension in the air rose. Sebastian cleared his throat, heading to the kitchen. "Beer? I was going to watch the game."

"Hockey or football?"

"Hockey," he called back. "The Golden Knights are playing the Bruins."

"Boston, huh." Well, it sounded better than hiding in her room. If he could get over their awkwardness for the night, all the better. "Okay, beer me. I'll just nip in the shower."

He'd tidied everything away when she came back in wearing sweats. Somehow wearing pyjamas felt a little too domestic. He'd laid some snacks on the table, and the hockey was in full flow. His eyes drifted to her when she entered, looking her up and down before meeting her eye. He lifted a bottle in welcome, and she took it, taking a seat next to him but without touching. He patted a blanket on the back of the couch, something she'd not noticed before. It was a little girlie for him.

"If you get cold," he said.

"Thanks," she muttered, turning her attention to the screen.

"Oh, come on! He should have made that one!"

Sebastian tutted, poking her in the thigh with a scowl. "Have you seen their goalie? He's not exactly tiny!"

"So? The goaltender wasn't even looking—he glanced behind him after the shot was taken! He should have got that one. Your team sucks!"

"Er…you mean our team. You live here, you support the Golden Knights, baby. It's the law."

She was sitting close now, her legs covered by the blanket she'd pulled over herself sometime in the second period. He wasn't about to tell her he'd bought it that day, along with a few other things he'd thought she might like around the place. He still didn't understand his purchases himself. Something had just come over him when he'd been out buying food.

Something about having someone in his life was changing him. He'd never had to care about another person before. His parents had barely cared for each other; growing up around them was all about what other people thought. What they had and what other people thought of them. Here, having her as his wife, he felt this new sensation of being accountable to another human. A person that didn't need him or rely on him. They just…made each other better in a lot of ways. Something about her energy made him sit up and take notice. Want to be better, especially now they were linked to everyone who knew them. Like his actions were a reflection of her too, and he wanted to avoid disappointing her.

When he'd looked around his place, it was like he was seeing how alone he was before. His apartment was nice, but not flashy. It was close to the hospital and convenient, but when he knew that Taylor was moving in, the starkness of his existence came to light for the first time. So he'd bought a few things. She didn't have to know. He'd never tell her. Geez, no. She might get the wrong idea, and they were already on a tenuous thread of working and living together as fake husband and wife.

The trouble was, sitting here on the couch arguing about hockey with her was the best time he'd had since…well, the last night he'd spent with her.

Don't think about that right now, Seb. It's not going to happen again.

It must have been her getting hurt that was

playing with his protective side. The medic in him. Yep, that was it. The lonely medic was just feeling some kind of fleeting attraction, which would pass when this marriage was over and she was out of his place, back to being the annoying colleague he loved to tease.

He watched as she sank the rest of her beer. “Another?” He went to get up, but her hand reached out to stop him. A mistake, because the spark of electricity from her touch zinged up his arm, and when he met her eye, he knew she felt it too. So much for avoiding her.

“Er…no,” she breathed, licking her lips. “Better not.”

She looked…nervous. Was she feeling this too? Since that night, breaking the touch barrier like they had, the lines had been blurred. Which brought his passing attraction to her right to the forefront. He thought he was alone in that, but the way she was looking at him now… It was just like that night at the altar. Right before his mouth had met hers.

He was done for the second she licked those lips. “Are you sure I can’t tempt you?”

Her chuckle was all nerves. “I’m sure you could, but it’s late. You have one though.”

He’d need a polygraph to testify who reached for who first. He didn’t know whether it was him or her, but one minute he was supposed to be heading to the fridge and the next his lips were on hers. His back hit the couch as she threw off the blanket and they were grabbing for each other. Her hands were in his hair, his hands snaking up the back of her top to find soft, bare skin. He pulled her closer, across the couch, until her thighs were sandwiching his, her core on his as he hardened instantly beneath her.

The hockey game continued but he couldn't have picked out a word. His head was full of Taylor—her scent, the way she felt, the way her tongue met his and danced with it. *It wasn't a fluke*, his elated, alarmed brain sang. Their night together wasn't a drunken one-off or an anomaly. This…thing between them, this passion and fire, it was still there. This time they weren't drunk or partying. They were fully aware of what was happening between them and still unable to control it.

Stop it, his rational brain told him, while his body pulled her closer. *This isn't a relationship. You don't even want one. Pull it together.*

His body didn't seem to be obeying, busy doing its own thing. He moved his hands to the front of her body and ran his thumbs over her bare nipples. *I just knew she didn't have a bra on under her sweats.* She moaned into his mouth, pushing further into his hands as he kissed the ever-loving hell out of her. He was lost, lost, lost…

His phone rang, and they sprang apart.

"Oh god." Taylor looked horrified and beautifully messed up. Her hair was ruffled, her top slightly lifted, and her face…? That gorgeous, sexy blush was all over her cheeks right now.

His inner alpha roared at the thought that he'd riled her up like that. *That's my damn wife*, it growled. "I'm sorry, I shouldn't have…"

The phone kept ringing and Sebastian wanted to throw it at the wall. When he made the mistake of reaching for it, Taylor ran. He heard her door slam, and he scowled down at the screen before answering.

"Patrick," he grumbled, his voice still thick with lust. "This better be life-and-death."

"Huh? I was just checking in—you didn't text me back earlier. How's life with the wife?"

Sebastian's gaze turned to the hallway, and her closed door.

"Living the domestic dream, pal." The final hockey buzzer sounded. His team had lost, and that wasn't the worst part of tonight. "I've gotta go. See you at work."

He was off the couch and at her door before he could even think of a reason not to do it. He was about to knock, when the door opened, and there she was. Stunning, beautiful. And not his. She couldn't be his, and he knew it. It would never work. They were not really married, or in love. They were frenemies at best, and this was never going to be anything else. He needed to stop it, once and for all. Ignore the cells in his body that were telling him to reach for her, to make her his. It wasn't the plan. It wasn't part of any plan, separate or apart. He couldn't let anything else get in the way of his residency. He needed to be smart, rational. Stoic, even in the face of everything his heart and body were seemingly intent on clueing him in on. He needed to shut this down, right the hell now.

"Taylor, I—"

"I know. We shouldn't have done that."

His heart came to a screeching stop in his rib cage. "No. Not a good idea."

"The worst, after getting drunk and getting married." Her nervous smile turned real, and she giggled. "Sorry. I guess I am still in shock about all that. It's just not like me."

"Me either. Maybe our alter egos are actually quite crazy."

"You make me crazy," she blurted, and his whole body reacted.

"I do?" He'd stepped closer, wanting so badly to know the answer. "In what way?"

"The same way I drive you mad, probably. You annoy me." She sighed, and he didn't miss the way she licked her lips when her gaze dropped to his. "And challenge me. And just now, on the couch…"

"You wanted me, didn't you?" *Admit it. Admit that I am not the only one confused as hell by this.*

It hadn't even been a week of marriage and he

couldn't get enough of her. He was so upset that morning when he'd woken up in the hotel room married to her. Except for the fact that he couldn't get the rest of the night out of his head. He'd never spent a night like that with a woman before, and just now? More of the same.

"I wanted you too."

"It's a bad idea," she said, pulling him closer by his shirt. "We hate each other. We will be divorced this time next year. Even if we both end up staying here, you will be my colleague and my ex-husband. That's not going to change. I want my career—anything else is not going to be in my future."

"Ditto," he told her. "I want the residency just as much as you do."

"Not possible," she refuted. "This has to be my next step. I've already messed up badly, I can't have things derail."

"So we stay on track." He pushed his hand through her hair and gripped the back of her neck. "But given we're stuck in this, playing the part, we might as well get something out of it too."

He was breathing hard, his whole body tingling to touch her. She was panting too, and he was hanging by a thread as he watched her consider his offer. Hell, he would dare her again if it came to it. *I dare you to let me take you, Taylor.*

"No strings, no feelings," she said eventually. "This is all it can be."

"Agreed. None." He tried to stop his breathing from sounding so ragged, but the pure lust surging through him was making it impossible. "Just two people who find each other sexy, but want nothing more."

"Professional."

He grinned, tightening his grip on her. "When am I ever anything but?"

"Brown?"

"Yeah?"

"Shut up and get in here."

CHAPTER NINE

"YOU SLEPT WITH him again?"

Taylor shoved her hand over Selina's mouth, nodding hello at Collette, who was quite possibly the nosiest nurse on the planet. They were on the OB floor, and perhaps it wasn't the best place to admit that she'd had the best sex of her life last night. Three times, if she was counting. Which she totally was, because she couldn't believe it had happened again.

Selina pulled her farther from their patient's room, still staying close enough to be there if she woke up. Dawn Rothwell was currently thirty-five weeks into a high-risk pregnancy. She had a congenital heart condition, which meant that her pregnancy was risky from the start. But Dawn was desperate to become a mother, and with Dr. Ashanda's extra care, bed rest and checkups, she had got to this point and was due to deliver in the morning by cesarean section.

Dr. Ashanda was fond of Dawn, as fond as she got with anyone, and had enlisted Taylor to monitor her. She was suffering from a touch of high blood pressure, triggered by worry and stress about her impeding delivery, so Dr. Ashanda had admitted her early to keep her off her feet and not focusing on all of the bad things that could happen. Her ECGs and echocardiograms were all normal, but everyone concerned was eager for her blood pressure to come down before her scheduled delivery. Especially because Dawn was doing this alone, having secured a sperm donor to have the child that she desperately wanted. The child that she was willing to risk her life to have.

Taylor had spent the last hour by her bedside, keeping her calm and distracting her from her worries. She'd been thrilled with herself when Dawn finally fell asleep. Unfortunately, that had left her time to chat to her friend, which she now realized was not the best idea.

"So what does it mean? Are you like, together for real now?"

"No! No. Of course not. It's not like that."

Selina's face was a picture of incredulity. "You having great sex with your husband isn't like that? Have you been on the gas and air? Of course it's like that!"

Taylor shushed her again, turning her attention to the patient chart. Selina pulled it from her grasp with a grin. "Tay, come on. I'm your best friend, not some idiot who came down in the last shower. I called this a long time ago. The chemistry between you two is next level. There is no way that you can stay married and live together now without feeling something. It's been what, a week? Admit it, you like him!"

"I do not, and I am not telling you anything again as long as I live."

Selina shot her a look and then laughed her head off.

"I'm going back to our patient," Taylor pouted.

"Can't handle the truth, eh? At least tell your mother! She keeps calling the landline at the apartment, and I'm running out of excuses for why you're not there when she knows you're not at work!"

Pausing at the doorway, she turned back to her friend.

"Listen, it's just…" Taylor began.

What was it exactly? Taylor couldn't say exactly, but she did know that last night, and in the early hours of this morning, they had enjoyed each other. Reached for each other in the dark and not even spoken a word before they were kissing again. Which was great, because they didn't need words, right? Talking led to confusion and awkward conversations, which she didn't want to have again. This was better. Far better. They were frenemies with benefits…or something.

"Just?" Selina pressed, that ever-knowing grin on her face.

"I don't know, but it's working so far, right?" She sighed heavily, feeling the weight of the responsibilities on her shoulders grow heavy. "I want that residency, Sel. I need it. For me, for my family. Anything else is just…not part of the plan. The plan that I've worked for years to pull off. I can't wreck it now, for anything. Life has a way of throwing a wrench in the works whenever it feels like it. I just want to have all my ducks in a row, feel secure. I don't need some man in the mix for any of that. I never did."

As Taylor walked back into the patient room, Dawn smiled at her sleepily.

"Sorry, I must have fallen asleep."

Taylor checked the monitors. Her oxygen levels and blood pressure were good, great even considering her condition and advanced pregnancy.

"You did right. Once the little one comes, there will be no sleeping. Your vitals are great. Blood pressure has dropped nicely."

Dawn rubbed her belly, a happy smile on her face. "Thankfully. I just want it to be tomorrow already. I can't wait to meet the little guy."

"You have any names yet?" Taylor consulted her chart, firing off a text message to Dr. Ashanda to keep her updated.

"I have a few, but several of the mothers in my

pre-natal group said that I'll know what works when I meet him, so we'll see. Oh. Ouch." Dawn sat upright, wincing in pain.

"What's wrong? Where is the pain?" Taylor checked the monitors, on high alert, but everything looked normal.

"My back," Dawn laughed. "Stand down. I think he's using my body as a springboard, that's all. Have you got any kids, with your husband?"

She looked down at the ring on her finger. "Nope. No kids. We're…er…both doctors, interns, so no babies for us."

"I thought that, once upon a time." Dawn shrugged, settling back against the pillows. "I did think I would be married by now, but that wasn't in the cards. You been married long?"

"Not long. We…sort of eloped."

"Oh, eloping is so romantic!" Dawn's grin dropped right off her face. "Oh god. I think…" The monitors beeped, her heartbeat now rapid. "Either I just peed myself or my water broke."

Taylor pulled back the covers, hitting the call button and coming to Dawn's side.

"Okay, Dawn. Your water broke. I've called for Selina to help."

"Oh god," she said and winced. "It's too soon, right? I can't deliver like this, right?"

"I'm right here." Taylor grabbed her hand. "You're not alone."

Selina came running in, and then everything happened at once. Dr. Ashanda was called, and the delivery team sprang into action.

"Heart rate is steady, but her blood pressure is rising."

Selina checked the baby, leaning in close and away from Dawn's ear. "Some signs of fetal distress."

Dr. Ashanda looked at the two women, and back at the monitors.

"Get me an OR, and a team. This operation is happening tonight."

The team rushed to take the monitors off the stands, placing them on the bed next to Dawn as Taylor stayed by her side.

"Dawn, we're going to take you to the OR now, bring forward your cesarean and make sure you deliver safely, okay? I need you to stay calm. Everything is going to be okay."

"You promise?" She was in a panic, gripping her stomach as if she could keep her baby safe just by holding him close. "I can't lose him. Not now."

Pulling the bed out of the room, the team started to run toward the OR floor. Taylor ran right alongside them, not letting go of Dawn's hand for one second.

"We have got you both, Dawn. Just stay calm and let me do the worrying, okay?"

For a moment, the two women stared at each other, a moment of pure trust passing between them.

"Okay," Dawn said. "I trust you."

When they got to the ER, Sebastian was there with a waiting operating team, gowned and ready. She rattled off Dawn's stats while the anesthetist prepped Dawn for the c-section. Sebastian nodded, getting to work while Dr. Ashanda scrubbed in.

"I'm staying in," Taylor told Dr. Ashanda when she noticed her standing with Dawn. "I can keep her calm."

Dr. Ashanda gave her a look, but her eyes behind the mask were kind.

"Good work, Dr. Cousins. Team, let's go. Patient's vitals are stable, time for this baby to meet the world."

"You okay?" Sebastian asked quietly, and she shot him a smile as one of the scrub nurses brought her a mask and gown. Dawn was calmer now, her grip a little less tense than before.

"Is that him?" she asked Taylor. She saw Sebastian's brows lift, one of them quirking upward in question.

"Yes," she laughed. "This is Sebastian, my husband."

Dawn smiled at him as he gave her a wave before getting back to work.

"He's cute," she giggled. "And those eyes! You two will make really cute babies." Sebastian turned to bat his lashes at them both, making Taylor roll hers. Dr. Ashanda stood at the table, ready to start cutting. Taylor gave her a nod of acknowledgment, turning back to Dawn and taking a seat on the stool next to her.

"Okay, Dawn. It's time for you to meet your son."

The Vegas night was still full of heat when they finally got out to the parking lot.

"That was amazing," Taylor breathed, looking up at the night sky and still feeling the high. "I still can't believe she named him after me."

Sebastian laughed, pulling her closer when she swayed on her feet.

"Neither can I. Sebastian is such a better name for a boy."

"Hey!" She went to swat him, but it fell short because her arms were exhausted. They went back to hanging like limp noodles by her side. "Taylor is an excellent name for a boy or a girl. You're just jealous."

"Sure," he scoffed. "Of course I am. Do you want to grab some food on the way home? Or I can order in."

"Order in. I smell like the OR, and I'm pretty tired." Her phone trilled in her bag, and her mother's name filled the screen. "Just give me a minute."

Stepping away, she steeled herself for yet another lying session.

"Hey, Mom!"

"Oh, you remember who I am! Hear that, Mom, my child remembers me!"

"Very funny, Mom, I'm sorry. I've been busy."

She looked back at Sebastian, who called "Thai?" to her. She made a gagging motion with her tongue, making him laugh. Putting her hand over the mouthpiece, she rolled her eyes.

"My cell provider," she told him, and he pulled a face back.

"I know," her mother said. "Too busy showering and taking out the trash, apparently. Every time I call you at home, Selina says you're busy doing the wildest things. Is everything okay?"

Damn it. This woman was like a bloodhound. She could smell avoidance a mile off.

"Everything's fine, Mom. I actually helped deliver a baby today, and the mother named him Tay—"

"Hey, wifey?" Sebastian called from behind her. "How about we get pizza on the way home, and watch the game on the couch?" Taylor's whole body tensed as she whirled around to Sebastian, her mouth dropping off. "What? No pizza? Not even pepperoni?" He waggled his brows, utterly oblivious to the utter crap storm he'd just unleashed. "I'll make it worth your while... What?"

He finally cottoned on to the fact that she was gesticulating wildly at him, but the damage was done. After the longest time of silence down the line, her mother finally spoke.

"Taylor, what the hell is going on? Did he just call you wife? Who is he?"

Taylor cringed to the tips of her toes. Game over. The Cousins women knew. She felt Sebastian touch her shoulder.

"You okay?" he asked, his face full of concern. "What's with the face?"

Covering the mouthpiece and ignoring her mother, who was currently relaying the bombshell to her grams, she made a slitting motion with her fingers across her throat, and Sebastian's brows shot to his hairline.

Well, at least I don't need to worry about getting divorced now. I'm definitely going to off my husband—if my mother doesn't kill me first.

CHAPTER TEN

After the night he'd accidentally outed their marriage to her mother, things got a little hairy. Taylor was stressed, and honestly he could see why. If his family found out about them, his life would be complicated too. They would no doubt have something to say about him having a Vegas quickie wedding, with a colleague no less. That would definitely not have fitted in with the Harrison reputation, whether he'd abandoned their surname or not. Her family was no doubt proud of their daughter; who wouldn't be? He couldn't blame her for not wanting to disappoint her family, especially when the whole thing was fake in the first place.

He knew her. She was buttoned up, organized. Professional. None of which described their current marital predicament. She'd withdrawn into herself, away from him. No doubt worrying about what her family thought, and juggling their fake life at work didn't ease the tension anyway. It took a solid week for her to speak to him properly outside of work, never mind come back to his bed. The fact was that sparring with each other only fueled the sexual tension between them. How he'd never noticed it before was laughable now. All of their competitiveness was still there, their rivalry, but now it had taken on a new life. One he was really enjoying, even though the impending divorce was starting to weigh heavily.

They both knew that this thing was just till the residency spots were announced. Once that was done, they would quietly divorce. If one of them didn't get a spot at the Valley and had to move, that would make things easier of course. If they both got their wish to stay in Vegas? Well, that would be a whole other plan to grapple with.

The last two weeks had been amazing. They were both on fire at work. Dr. Ashanda had never been happier with their performance. And Taylor was seemingly impressed with his too, because she had developed a habit of ripping his clothes off the second they got home. The other night, they didn't even make it out of the car. His new wife was an absolute smoke show, but he was just waiting for the other shoe to drop. That shoe being the fact that they hadn't had one conversation about the future, or what it might mean. He was rapidly turning into a guy who was going to ask the question "Where are we going with this?"

Sebastian and Patrick were in their usual bar and the hockey game was on but even his favorite team wasn't providing a distraction. "I think I might like her," he blurted out over the noise of the bar. "I don't want to. I don't even know when it started, really. I mean, I guess there was always something there, I just didn't see it. Or I ignored it. Who knows. The point is, I'm screwed, Patrick. I like her, and I can't seem to brush that feeling off."

Patrick almost choked on his beer. "What? You like someone? Who? You know you're still married, right? I thought you would be too busy to look elsewhere."

Sebastian drained his beer and reached for the next. He'd dragged Patrick out tonight because he needed to talk to someone, and he was fast realizing that Patrick with his short attention span probably wasn't the best person to spill his guts to.

"I'm talking about *her*. I like my wife. A lot."

"Well, that's a good thing, right? Since you're constantly clawing at each other like a couple of wild animals."

"What?" Sebastian almost broke the glass bottle in his grasp. "How do you know that?"

Patrick shrugged, ripping off the label on his own IPA. "Selina might have said something. Taylor told her. Which kind of hurt, man. I thought we were buddies!"

"It's a little different. Women talk. I'm not going to tell you the details of my sex life." Which was off-the-charts, next-level amazing. Taylor had pretty much spoiled him for all other women. "Besides, the sex isn't the problem."

"Obviously. So what's the problem? You fancy your wife, you live together. Isn't that how it's supposed to be?"

Sebastian hung his head. "Yeah, but it's still fake. It's going to end once the residencies get announced. We won't need to be married anymore. There will be no reason to keep up the game we're playing when we get the jobs. We're only keeping this charade up so that our silly drunken mistake doesn't hurt our shots at getting residency spots. We only have a short amount of time before that happens. Dr. Ashanda has already finished the other interviews—for some reason she's been on a mission to announce early." Which would have been amazing in another universe, just not this one, when he needed time to figure out what was going on and how to keep Taylor in his life.

Patrick took another sip, deep in thought. "So, stay married then. You don't have to divorce her. You could tell her. She might feel the same, bro. You never know till you ask."

"No. She doesn't. I let slip to her family, by accident. She was mortified. She told her mother about the marriage, but only because she had to. She told her it was fake too. If she had feelings, she would have said something by now. But instead I can feel her pulling away from me. She doesn't want this, and I don't even know what I want. Not for sure. This was definitely not part of the plan, for either of us. Sex is one thing, but I think I might want more, and she definitely doesn't. Believe me."

"In-laws, eh? Getting serious."

Sebastian groaned, fixing Patrick with one of his very best glares that he used to reserve for Taylor. "Are you listening to me? She had to tell them—I outed her by accident."

"I can relate," Patrick quipped. "It happens."

Sebastian snorted. "Whatever. It doesn't matter, either way. She's not into this, whatever it is. She doesn't talk about anything serious, and she keeps her family separate from me. It's…bothering me. More than I thought it would. I didn't think that she was into me, other than the physical side, but when we're together…"

His mind drifted to the night before. Her lying in his arms after they'd made love. And it was love that they'd made, not sex. Sometimes it was hot and heavy, shedding their clothes, all teeth and tongues and heavy pants, but other times, it was slow touches, quiet moans and soft caresses. Like last night. She'd gone to bed early, exhausted after a long surgery. He'd cleaned up the kitchen and headed to bed, quietly gutted that she'd gone to sleep in her own room. But when he opened his bedroom door, there she was. Asleep in his bed.

She looked like she belonged there, and he just couldn't help himself. He'd slipped under the covers and kissed her cheek, not expecting her to wake up. The second his lips had touched her skin, those beautiful eyes of hers had opened, and he was a goner for her. They'd never said a word, undressing the other slowly in the dark. When he'd entered her, their eyes locked, he knew that this was more for him. Had been more for him for a long time. Sure, their forced proximity and marriage had thrust them together against their will, but it didn't mean that what he was feeling wasn't real. Hadn't been real, for a long time.

If he was honest with himself, Taylor Cousins had rocked his world since they'd met. His very own, exasperating, infuriating goddess of a woman. *How had he not seen this coming?* Had he really been so blind, so focused on proving that he wasn't the man he'd been raised to be? And what if when she knew the truth about who he was, she didn't want him? She hated everything his background embodied. If she rejected him once she knew the truth, it would kill him. She was the one person who had been close to him, brought him out of his shell. Challenged him. If she left him alone now, the pain would be indescribable. He hadn't planned for any of this, but losing it? The thought of that churned his guts.

But then this morning, she'd acted like nothing had changed. Nothing different had happened, and it had felt like a rejection. Like he was just a tool to be used. A convenience. A toy to be played with till it didn't fit the agenda. He didn't want that. He wanted to be someone she wanted more from. They were unique together, like they fit. He wanted her to want to keep him, even when she knew everything.

Man, my childhood did more of a number on me than I ever realized.

It stung, her acting like the moments in bed together meant less to her than anything he was feeling. It wasn't like he was expecting to feel this way, but here he was. Alone in his turnabout seemingly. It made him want to try harder, yet he feared that it still wouldn't be enough. He'd been trying to care for her, make her lunches, ensure she was fed and rested, comfortable in his home. He lived for the smiles she gave him whenever she realized he'd done something for her.

She did things for him too, leaving articles marked in journals that she knew he was researching. Changing his sheets and straightening up the place. Whenever she brought him a coffee at work, he felt like a conquering king. It just wasn't enough anymore, and when he thought of her bringing someone else a cup of Joe one day, his stomach twisted. Was that going to happen? If they both got the residencies at the Valley like they wanted, would he be destined to watch his ex-wife living a life that didn't include him?

Patrick slid closer in the booth, patting him on the shoulder and dragging him out of his head.

"Geez, man, I never realized you had it so bad. I kinda figured it was just some angry kink."

"She's not a kink," Sebastian laughed, shoving Patrick playfully with his shoulder. "She's my wife."

Patrick's chuckle was loud, even over the din of the bar.

"Wow. Sebastian Brown in love. This is new."

"I'm not..." He trailed off, digesting the words. "That's not what this is. Right?"

Patrick raised his bottle, clinking it against Sebastian's. "Who knows, man, but if you feel like this, it's got to be worth pursuing, right?"

"It's not that easy. I'm not even sure she feels like this."

"Selina thinks she does."

"Yeah?" Sebastian's ears pricked up at that little nugget of information. "What did she say?"

"Well, you know Taylor. Man, she's like a vault, but Selina thought a long time ago that this fighting thing you two have was foreplay. She's noticed a change in her, and Selina doesn't miss a trick. You want another beer?"

"Sure," he murmured, barely registering Patrick shuffling off to the bar. Was that right? If Selina could read the attraction in her friend too, there might be something to this, right? Maybe he could test the waters before he got into this any further.

Pulling out his phone, he fired off a text.

Hey. What are you up to?

Patrick was back with the beers before his phone pinged with her response.

Just brushing up for my surgery tomorrow. Did you want something?

Wow. A bit cold after last night.

Just checking in. I'll see you later.

Ok. I'll be asleep, so see you in the morning. Going in early, so don't bother knocking for me before you set off.

Patrick passed him another beer, and he drank it like he'd just come out of the desert, before reaching for one of the shots he'd brought. The hit of alcohol on the back of his throat did nothing to dull the pain in his chest. It was all for show after all. He couldn't even call her on it. They'd agreed to continue with the fake marriage for the sake of their careers, they'd agreed to have no-strings-attached sex.

The complicated lies and image management

had begun to remind him of his family growing up. In public he was the heir, the cherished son trained to continue the legacy. Behind closed doors he was the rebellious disappointment. When he didn't fit in with their agenda, he was discarded. Or would have been, if he hadn't walked away first, changing his surname to underline his independence.

Taylor was a woman who knew what she wanted, and it looked like that didn't include him. It was triggering, to say the least. Taylor going from hot to cold was giving him whiplash, and he was fast realizing that he wanted this, and that meant no more hiding. No more pretending. It was choking him up. Taylor was unlike any woman he'd ever met, and he was…beguiled. *I have to take my shot.*

If he told her the truth, about everything, then he would know. Once and for all. If she rejected him, then he'd stick to the plan, get divorced and try to keep himself together for the residency spot. He just…had to know whether Taylor was really his, and not just on paper.

CHAPTER ELEVEN

TAYLOR WAS WITH SELINA, getting the clinic area prepped for one of their least favorite days. Today, all manner of patients would come in with suspicious moles, cysts, pus-filled boils and just about every other skin condition that could be found in a medical textbook. Interns got this duty because it was great practice, requiring all manner of testing and surgical skills, but in reality it was grunt work and they knew it. Still, it was necessary.

Taylor herself had diagnosed a few patients with early forms of skin cancer, and the look on her patients' faces reminded her of the day her mother was told that the odd little lump in her breast was possibly going to kill her. By the time she went to get it checked out it was already in one of her lymph nodes and Taylor knew what that meant. It still terrified her even now to think about it. About how her grams had wept in the kitchen when she thought no one could hear. How much she hated her father for not being there to help her mother, even though he'd shown his true colors and left a long time before. Thankfully. He wouldn't have been a help in that situation anyway, and Taylor had taken charge of everything. Including the financial burden. Her mother had to quit work, her grandmother was retired, so they stuck together and struggled through it.

Without a man in sight, they'd survived. Were surviving. They were almost there. The medical debt was a constant reminder of what she needed to achieve, and she couldn't wait for the day when she was free from it all. She needed to be free of a lot of things. Her brain was crammed too full at the moment. Mostly with thoughts of Sebastian, and the fact that she was starting to really, really like him. It wasn't just sex to her anymore. She knew him, knew his touch and the way he looked out for her in little ways. The way he looked at her had changed too, and she knew she was making heart eyes at him half the time too.

It was freaking her out, this connection between them. Physical, mental, emotional. She didn't want any of this. Barely a few weeks ago he'd just been the hot, annoying intern who was also the bane of her life. Now? Well, now she was dreading him bringing up their divorce, because the thought of it made her feel…out of sorts. Strangely alone, and that was a whole new thing for her to get her head around.

She was supposed to be focusing on the residency, not whether her husband wanted to try the whole marriage thing for real. Risking a man being part of her life for real terrified her, especially with the baggage she carried that he wasn't even aware of. He was financially stable—how would he feel when she told him about the medical debt, about the years of scrimping and saving? They were so different, so much could go wrong, and that's if they even ended up in the same state after internship. Nope. It was too much.

So of course she was burying the whole thing altogether. She'd been avoiding him for the past week, yet sleeping in her own bed in the spare room just felt wrong. Any bed felt wrong without him in it, but the last night they'd spent together, something had shifted. The eye contact, the synchronicity as they'd made love in his bed was good. Too good. It felt like something she could do for the rest of her life, and the thought of losing it, or trying and failing down the line, scared the ever-loving hell out of her. The next night, when he'd texted her from the bar, she'd reread his message over and over, looking for some sign that he was feeling it too, but found nothing more than a friendly check-in. She'd crawled out of his bed and into her own, made it clear that she was going to be asleep.

She was a grown-up, of course. An accomplished, clever doctor with an independent, busy life, but lately? She was a wife, someone who looked for her husband in hospital corridors and felt the butterflies when she set eyes on his face. She should just talk to him, have the conversation—feel him out at least, but whenever she thought about what to say, her whole throat closed up. She was considering booking an appointment with an ENT specialist at this point, it was happening so often.

So because she couldn't get her words out, she had chosen the other option. To avoid him as much as possible and throw herself into work. Which was also the method she was using to deal with the matriarchs in her life. Neither method was going particularly well. Her mother and grandmother were constantly blowing her phone up, and Sebastian kept shooting her looks that she couldn't decipher.

"Residencies are going to get announced any day now. Dr. Fleming has been extra nice to me, and I can't figure out if it's because I got the spot or he knows I didn't and doesn't want to tip me off." Selina huffed, pushing an errant strand of hair back into place as she stooped to get supplies from the lower shelves in the medical storage closet they were both currently ensconced in. Another thing that only served to remind her of Sebastian.

"Mmm-hmm." Taylor pulled out another pack of gauze, layering it on top of the pile of surgical equipment already on the trolley.

"I mean, I think I'm a sure thing. He was in a

pretty bad mood during the interviews, which is usually a sure sign that he'd not been impressed."

"Yeah, sure. No doubt."

"Also, I think I'm in love with Patrick and want to have his giant, goofy babies. I was thinking we could pop out our own football team, turn them all into doctors."

"Sounds good to me."

"Taylor! I knew you weren't listening to me! What's up with you?"

Taylor sagged against the trolley. *Busted.* "Sorry. It's just…the stress of the residency announcements."

"You are a sure thing, both you and Sebastian. Try again."

"Well, my mother and Grams are bugging me about my marriage."

"When don't they bug you? You don't normally crack under their interrogation. I'm not buying it."

"Fine. It's Sebastian."

Selina grinned. "What did he do, leave his boxer shorts on the bathroom floor? Pee on the toilet seat?" She waggled her brows suggestively. "Give you too many back-to-back orgasms?"

"No, he…didn't really do anything. I just think we shouldn't have had sex again, that's all. It's made things…confusing." When she finally looked her friend in the face, Selina's expression was nothing short of gleeful. "Sel, don't gloat. I'm in hell."

"Naked, sweaty, sexy hell. I totally called this. Patrick owes me a bottle of tequila."

"You've talked to Patrick about this?"

"No, not the specifics, obvs! I did tell him that I thought that you two might end up together though."

Taylor snorted, but it sounded fake even to her ears. "We are not going to get together. He doesn't want that, and anyway, he's very well off. I'm… not, and won't be for a long time. He owns his place for a start. Mortgage free. I barely have anything left over each month after renting a room from you! He doesn't know everything about my family… I know pretty much nothing about his. Plus we get on each other's nerves half the time, and the other half we're—"

"Ripping each other's clothes off and mooning over each other?"

"It's more than that though. I don't know, something's changed lately. I feel…weird about the future."

"So tell him!"

Selina dumped the rest of the supplies onto the cart and dragged her friend to the door.

"I can't tell him," Taylor explained. "I don't even know how I feel yet. Not really. I can't put it into words, and we're stuck together for now. That's been enough of an adjustment as it is. You know me, Sel, I don't do the hearts-and-flowers stuff. I think relationships are a distraction, and this one—whatever it is—is definitely distracting me. Plus, I might get the bottle to spill everything and then he could just not want any of it. I don't exactly make a habit of sharing my life, Sel. Can you imagine how awful it would be if I blurted it out to him, and he laughed in my face?"

"Sebastian wouldn't do that. He's not a monster, Tay. I'm sure he has his own baggage too. I see the way he looks at you. That's not a guy who isn't interested. Make him a meal tonight and feel him out. If you get a bad vibe from him, then you can always pull back."

That wasn't the worst idea. They were both off shift at the same time.

"Maybe," she muttered. "If he offers me a lift home tonight, I'll talk to him. That'll be my sign from the universe."

They headed up to the clinic, and Taylor was on her second patient of the day when Sebastian came over to her. She was dealing with a regular in the clinic, a sweet elderly woman called Abigail Winters, who frequently came in with sun damage to her face. After years of living in the Florida sunshine, she'd had a patch of skin turn cancerous, and now she came in for regular check-ups and mole checks. Given that she was also a survivor of breast cancer some years before, the woman was vigilant with changes in her skin. Moving to Vegas had been part of her retirement plan, and she now lived with her son in a granny annex she loved.

"So, your mole has started bleeding?"

Abigail bit her lip, a slow nod her only reply. Taylor patted her arm, leaning in close to meet her eye. "It doesn't necessarily mean anything, and your last blood results came back normal. We can take a sample and get it to the lab to be sure, but I'm not overly concerned. Okay?"

Abigail smiled fully for the first time since walking into the clinic. "Okay dear, thank you. You're so lovely." She reached for her hand and froze when she felt something under her glove. "Oh, you're married! Congratulations!"

"Thank you," a cool, deep voice said. Taylor turned to see Sebastian standing there, his smile sincere and utterly adorable. "We're very happy."

Abigail gave him a none-too-subtle once-over, and winked at Taylor.

"A handsome doctor too! You make a lovely couple. I hope you're looking after her well. She's my favorite doctor. You're very lucky."

"Oh, I know." Sebastian grinned. "I can't believe she's my wife half the time. Honey?"

Taylor felt like her whole body was on fire. He hadn't been this close for a while, and she could smell him. With his scent and his kind words, she was about half a minute away from dragging him to the nearest closet and begging him to keep her.

"Yes, darling?" she trilled, recovering well

enough to get her words out. She knew her face was flushed though, and the look in his eyes told her that he was well aware.

"I just came to ask if you were still meeting me in the parking lot after shift? We can go home together."

There it was. The sign she told Selina she'd wait for. *Crap.*

"Sure," she told him, feeling like her heart was going to beat out of her chest. "Sounds good, baby."

CHAPTER TWELVE

WHEN SHE FINALLY mustered the courage to leave the locker room, Sebastian was waiting at the car for her. Two to-go cups in his hands, he looked gorgeous leaning against the hood of his car. She sometimes forgot how huge he was, how imposing and sexy a figure he cut, but she was well aware of it now. Her whole mouth was dry, and if she pulled at her fingers anymore, she was going to rip them off at the knuckle.

"Hey." He grinned, a hesitantly boyish smile that melted her heart to see.

When had these feelings for him changed? Once upon a time she hated to see his ridiculous face, and now he was pretty much her favorite person. The question of what he was to her loomed large. Would her baggage be an issue if she told him? Would it still feel the same if it was real, with no one to fool? Would he understand that she lived differently to him, and not just financially? He had no family, but hers were so important to her, and she had obligations that he didn't. Even the car he was leaning against was worth more than her savings, which didn't mean much of course. A remote-control radio car would clean that out, what with the insurance payments and the meager existence she was living.

He'd made that better too. The drop in costs, especially since Selina had insisted that she didn't need to pay rent for a place she wasn't staying in, had made life a little better. Still, she had a long way to go, and if she let him in and it didn't work out, would that mean another mess to sort out down the line along with a messy divorce?

"Thanks for coming," he said. "I didn't think you would accept the ride. You haven't been… close lately."

"Well, you didn't really give me a choice," she chided, no heat behind her retort. "My patient was kind of listening to the whole thing."

He came to open her door before she could reach for the handle. "Well, you're here now. Hot chocolate. Figured it was too late for coffee."

He'd brought her a drink too, one he knew she liked to have after a busy day. Another little way in which he cared for her. It made the words clog in her throat.

He pulled out of the parking lot, heading for home, but he didn't say anything. Didn't turn the radio on. She could feel him watching her, but she kept her eyes on the road. Her heart was hammering in her rib cage like a steel drum, but she was frozen in her seat.

"You okay?" he asked eventually. "You've been avoiding me."

"I haven't," she lied.

Sebastian reached across the space, covering her ever-moving hands with his.

"You have, Taylor. You're pulling at your fingers like you always do when you're stressed, and you haven't looked me in the face for what, a week? Longer? I don't understand what's going on. Have I done something?" He'd slowed to a stop in traffic, and she felt him reach for her jaw, pull her eyes to his. "Do you regret sleeping together? Because I don't."

"You don't?"

His brows furrowed and his grip on her jaw tightened just a touch before he had to release her when the lights changed. "No. I don't regret any of it, but I don't want to stress you out. I think we need to talk, properly."

She knew that they did, but she was so scared. Everything in her rational brain was telling her to pull back, to rage against what she was feeling and go back to the old days when Sebastian Brown was just the fly in her medicated ointment.

"I'm here for you, Taylor. Whatever you need."

Something sparked in her brain. What if she invited him to meet her family? A crazy idea, but it might just work. He would see for himself that they were from different worlds. That this whole thing between them was not meant to be. It might just put him off her when he realized how ill-suited they really were, and then she wouldn't have to deal with this. Any of it. *It could work. My family already know the truth. It wouldn't be hurting them. They've been bugging me about my fake husband for weeks anyway.*

"You really mean that? You'd help if I asked?"

His huge brown eyes glittered in the dark as he turned his full attention to her once more.

"Name it."

"Okay. Tomorrow, our day off? Come and meet my family."

CHAPTER THIRTEEN

"WHY ARE WE doing this again?" She was sweating. He could see it dripping down the nape of her neck as they stood on her mother's porch. It was more than the Vegas heat that had her perspiring. She was losing it. She'd not slept a wink all night, but Sebastian was taking the whole thing in his stride. He was happy at the prospect of being vetted by his fake wife's family. He wanted to show her that he could do this, that their lives could mesh together. He would never do this with his family, but he was happy to do this for her. With her.

"Because you asked me to, and your family is worried that your husband is a bad man who is corrupting you." He lowered his gaze to her lips. "And on that one, they are half right." When her eyes bulged, he chuckled, dropping a kiss on her forehead as if it was the most natural thing in the world. "Come on, stop picking at your hands. It will be fine, I promise."

"You didn't need to bring all that, you know."

He was laden with gifts. Wine, flowers, chocolates. He'd even bought them a set of piping bags, because of course he'd listened to Taylor and knew that they were both keen bakers. "They know we're not really married."

"I have a marriage certificate that begs to differ on that one."

"You know what I mean. They won't buy this act."

"Good." He grinned, adjusting the gifts in his arms to press the doorbell. "Because I'm not selling one. I am pretty sure I'm growing on you, for one thing."

"Oh yeah," she scoffed, rolling her eyes. "I'm madly in love with you, Dr. Brown."

"I knew it," he murmured, just as the door opened and the two Cousins women filled the doorway. *Showtime. Time to get my husband game face on.*

"Hello! You must be Sebastian!"

"Oh, he's handsome, Taylor! You never said he was so hunky!"

They were ushered into the house with all the diplomacy of a swarm of locusts. Her mother took the gifts from him while Grams practically ripped the jacket from his back.

"Er...hi." Sebastian smiled. "The gifts are for you both. As a thank-you for dinner."

"That's so nice! Isn't it nice, Sandra?" her mother commented.

"Lovely! Come through, don't stay in the hall. Dinner won't be long. Drink?"

Sebastian flashed Taylor a told-you grin before turning his megawatt smile to her mother. "That would be great, thanks."

The pair of them followed the two women into the lounge, where Grams promptly got the whiskey bottle out. She only did that for special guests. *What the heck?*

"Grams, he's driving." Taylor eyed the bottle. "I'll have one though."

The next half hour was excruciating. By the time they sat down at the dinner table, Taylor was on her second drink and feeling just a little rattled. *What is going on here? I thought they were going to go in on us, tell us what a mistake this is. How a fake relationship is bad news for both of us.*

"It's a lovely house you have here," he complimented as the two women filled his plate with enough meat and vegetables to feed a small village. "It's so warm and welcoming."

"Thank you, Sebastian," her mother simpered. "We like it. The garden's a real sun-trap. Plenty big enough for the two of us, though we do miss Taylor."

"It's a little tidier though," her grams teased.

"Our girl here was always leaving her medical books around the place."

"Oh, she still does that," Sebastian laughed. "I don't mind though, my place was pretty stark before she moved in."

Sandra shook her head. "I still can't believe you two got married and live together."

Taylor almost choked on her beef. "Oh, come on, Mom, you know it's not really like that."

Sebastian cleared his throat. "Well, technically that's all true. We are married, and we do live together." When Taylor looked at him, his expression was off. Like he was mad that she'd pointed out the obvious. "I call you wifey. Work thinks we're together. I don't know what we have differs from a 'real' marriage. Do you?"

She wanted to correct him, but she didn't have a leg to stand on. They had been sleeping together until recently. They had seen each other naked, a lot. He'd touched every part of her body, and she his. *Was this a real marriage?*

Her grams brought the charged silence to an end. "He's got you there, sweetheart. Does your family know about you two?"

It was an innocent question, but she sensed the change in him instantly. He was suddenly very interested in his meal.

"Grams! Don't interrogate him," she chided, feeling an overwhelming surge of protectiveness toward him.

"No, it's fine." He reached for her hand across the table, but she dodged it by reaching for her glass. His fist clenched before he took it back. "Er…no, my family don't know about Taylor. I don't have anything to do with them. Our outlook on life doesn't exactly align. It's just me now. Well, Taylor and I." He looked her full in the face, his gaze turning to determination. "That's all I need. I know that this whole marriage thing was somewhat unconventional, but Taylor is important to me. She makes me a better doctor, and a better man. I know you've been worried, but I know how important your family are to each other. Just because I don't have mine in my life by choice, that doesn't mean I won't look after her, for as long as we are together."

"Oh." Grams looked devastated. "That must be hard. Of course, Taylor is your family now, and us. Fake marriage or not."

Sandra was nodding in earnest. Both women were looking at Sebastian as though he hung the moon. Taylor wasn't far behind them. His words, his sincerity, they felt so real. She wanted it to be real. She had no idea he felt like that, hadn't thought much about him being alone. He must have been so lonely, living on his own and only having Patrick and his work colleagues to rely on. He'd always seemed so tailored and polished, put together.

"Exactly," Sandra said. "We didn't have the

usual family dynamic either. I'm sure you know that Taylor's father isn't in the picture. It's just been us three, until you came along. She's been avoiding us, but we can tell she's been happier lately. It's good, knowing that someone is looking out for her for once." Sandra ignored the daggers her daughter was throwing her. "My Taylor has always been a good girl, but stubbornly independent. She looked after me and Grams when I was sick, and she still helps out with all the financial—"

"Mom," Taylor cut in, her laugh awkward and too loud. "Sebastian doesn't need to know all that. We got through it, okay? You're better now, and once I get this residency, everything will be perfect. I can stay in Vegas, just like we always planned."

Sebastian was watching them, his fork slack in his hand. She hated feeling so vulnerable in front of him, on show. He didn't have to look after anyone, or worry about anything. If they got together for real, he'd be dragged into all of this. The family obligations and the debt. She had thousands left to pay, even with the meager extra money she had been managing to pay since they got married. What if he wanted to buy a house, or start a family? Sure, the residency money was good, but she still had a lot of work to do and her credit rating had taken a hit over the years.

Despite what he was telling her and her family, the facts didn't change, and if she didn't get the residency, she would have to leave anyway. Or perhaps he would. Any kind of relationship would be impossible with the hours and the distance. And that was after she got out of her own way and fully trusted him to be a life partner. She really liked him, but it was so fast, so foreign to her. So many ways that they could try this and fail. With all that pressure, how was she supposed to concentrate on her residency, on getting the rest of the money together?

For the millionth time, she talked herself out of hoping for something that she'd never wanted in the first place. These feelings were destined to be like her marriage: something that was going to end. Her time with Sebastian as her husband had an expiration date, and she needed to stick to the plan. If she lost sight of everything that she had worked for, then Sebastian would have even less reason to want to stay around.

The whole reason they were in this predicament was the fact that work had brought them together. Without that, would she still feel the same? It was just too risky, too scary. Sometimes life just didn't work out like some love story. People left, they got sick, they grew apart. She knew that better than anyone.

Realizing that the whole table was watching

her, she plastered on a smile and raised her glass. "Anyway, cheers to a nice meal, and for good company!"

The drive home was quieter than she'd imagined it would be. Sebastian had been the perfect fake husband the whole time, and after the awkward dinner conversation, her grams had taken charge. Ever the entertainer, she'd started telling a story about the scandals at her bridge club, and whatever tension had been present seemed to dissolve into small talk and lighter subjects. They'd left in a shower of hugs and enthusiastic goodbyes, and Sebastian was made to promise to come for dinner again soon. Shockingly, the two older Cousins women were rooting for their little ruse, which made Taylor question herself all over again.

Once they were alone in the car, she realized that it might just be her that was putting on a front. Having charmed both women, she thought he'd be smug at the very least. Instead he seemed worried about something. She spotted him looking her way a few times when the car stopped at a light, or in traffic, and she couldn't work out why. Was it feeling too real now? They didn't agree to involving families, after all. Was her crazy plan to make him see that they were different actually working? If it had, she didn't know how to feel about it. She wanted to feel nothing at all. It was far easier that way, as when Sebastian

Brown wasn't the reason her whole stupid world had turned upside down.

When they got back to his apartment building, he opened her car door as usual and once they were inside, he headed straight for the kitchen.

"Are you okay?" she asked after watching him drain a full glass of water. He refilled his glass, and motioned to ask if she wanted one. She nodded, coming to get it. "You were quiet in the car on the way back. I know it was a bit much to ask, spending time with my family like that." She wanted to ask him whether his words were true back there, what he felt now he'd seen her world, but she would never voice the burning feeling deep in her gut.

"I loved it," he said, coming to stand in front of her. "Your family's lovely. I just didn't realize that things had been so tough for you all, with your dad leaving and your mom getting sick. I get why you work so hard for the residency now, even more than I did before. Leaving them would be really hard on you all."

"Yeah, it would, but that's not going to happen. I've been working for this for too long to let anything derail it now."

He smiled, but it didn't quite reach his eyes. "To gaining residency," he said softly, lifting his glass and chinking it against hers. "I hope we both get what we want, when everything's said and done."

She took a sip, wondering what he meant by that. The lines had been blurring between them so much lately, it was hard to see clearly.

"I'm sure we will. Once the residencies are announced. I feel like we're both firmly in the running."

"Yeah, I think so too," he agreed. "But that brings other problems with it. If we're both still in Vegas, we'll have things to talk about."

"I know," she admitted. Was he going to mention divorce now? "I guess we will, if it comes to it."

He sighed. "But we don't have to know all the answers right now. We can figure this out, once we know where things lie at work." He came over to her, tucking her into his huge body and making her feel so comfortable she melted into him. "We can just be together, in this moment. Keep working and trust that the rest of it will just work out." She laughed, which made his chest rumble with a chuckle of his own. "What? Too corny?"

"No, I just never thought we would be like this. I used to dream about ways to take you down, Brown."

"Oh yeah?" He dropped a kiss on the top of her head before gripping the back of her neck to tilt her head to his. "Dirty ways? Because I have a few things I'd like to try. You've not been near me lately. I want to change that, if you'll let me."

He was distracting her, and they both knew it.

The thing was it was working. She could just kiss him right now. Let him take her to bed and just be together for a few hours, in their place. Their bed. She was desperate for him; being so close and feeling his warm, strong body against hers was torture. Tonight wasn't the problem though. The morning would be. How she'd feel waking up in his arms, seeing him at work knowing that just hours before they'd spent the whole night lost in each other. She just couldn't do it. Not anymore. It was time for reality.

"I don't think that's a good idea," she murmured when his lips were a whisper away from hers. She felt him freeze, his hands still on her hips where they'd come to rest just mere moments earlier. "We need to stop."

He backed off immediately, his head dipping to meet her eye. "Tell me why. You've been distant a while now, Taylor. I don't understand. I like you. In fact, I was past 'like' a while ago. We're already together in all the ways that count. You took me to meet your family today, and that meant something to me. Why can't we just do this for real?"

No, no, no. He was saying everything she'd hoped he would. The high-alert siren in her head was going off and screaming in her ears as she stepped away from him. *Fight or flight time.*

"For real? Are you joking? We both know that

this whole thing has been a total nightmare from the beginning! I don't even know you!"

"Of course you know me, Taylor." He laid his closed fist on his chest, right over his heart. "This started off as a dare gone too far. Sure. I thought so too, at the time. I mean, I always thought you were attractive, but you were also a colossal pain in my ass. I thought that you were the most annoying, talented woman on the planet, but I never felt romance before that night. When we woke up married, I was horrified. Because I had just had one of the best nights of my life, and it was with you. We hated each other, and I figured it was just a drunken mistake. A blip. It is Vegas, it happens. So if I'd ended up divorced, it wasn't like I had anyone to tell. Then Patrick opened his stupid mouth, and everyone knew our secret. But I figured we could get through it. Make the best of things—try not to kill each other until we got the residencies and then leave each other behind."

"I thought the same!" she agreed, glossing over the parts that hurt. "I never wanted to be married to you. I didn't think I would date *anyone*, let alone that."

"Me neither." He smiled, his expression pained. "Till I got to really know you. To understand you."

She was barely breathing, not sure whether she wanted to know the answer to her next question but desperate to ask it anyway. It wouldn't make a difference, she warned herself. Whatever he said now was only going to be more to pore over later, to torture herself with.

"And then?"

"And then we worked and lived together. Made a life. Spent nights together. Made love. A life. Hockey nights on the couch, smushed under a blanket. Pizza nights. Waking up with you all sleepy and soft, with my body wrapped around you. Going to the grocery store together and arguing over which toilet paper to buy. Your hair, clogging up the shower drain. You leaving notes in my textbooks, and your tea bags on the countertop. All the little things you invaded my life with, and I've grown to anticipate them. Look for these little pieces of you peppered into my life. Your stuff with my stuff in this apartment, my ring on your finger. I grew to tolerate it, and then like it." He swallowed audibly. "Love it even. I guess I just stopped thinking about this as fake."

"But it is fake, Sebastian. We come from different worlds. I have so much baggage. I never wanted to be in a relationship. I never needed someone that way. I still don't. I'm driven, and stubborn, and I learned from an early age that being in love with someone was trouble. Life's not a rom-com, it's a drama at best. A horror show at worst. It's too hard. My family need me, and I've sacrificed a lot for them. I can't let anything distract me from the plan. My plan. Our plan."

"So what? None of that life stuff would have to change. I don't want you to uproot your life, Taylor—I just want to stay in it. I wouldn't say your family is a burden. They're great people, and I only want to help. You know we work well together, drive each other to be better. I don't want you to put aside your career for me any more than you want that from me. I don't want you chained to some sink, I want you as you are, Taylor. Operating with me. Fighting at work with me. Snuggling on the couch after a hard day at the hospital. We have all that! I just want it to be real. Is that so bad? Please, come and sit down on the couch with me. Let's at least talk. Please?"

When she didn't move, he loped over to the couch, patting the seat cushion next to him. She took a deep breath. Here it was. She had to tell him about the debt, the reason she needed to stay in Vegas and earn more money while still trying to chase her dreams. The terror she felt at letting her family down and not achieving everything that she had worked her ass off for. The fact that she didn't know how to do this for real, because she wasn't built that way. She was the provider, the strong one, and she was used to doing things on her own.

Love changed people, made them take each other for granted. Made them dismiss what they needed or what their partner needed till both people were angry and trapped in something they should never have started.

When he shot her a pleading look, she relented, sitting down and trying to ignore his proximity. She needed to stay on point, get this out. Getting lost in him was the reason she was here in the first place.

"My family is not the burden. The medical debt my mother ran up while fighting cancer is. The fact is that my father and grandfather were both asses who didn't treat their women right and dulled their light. I resolved a long time ago that it wouldn't be me, and when Mom got sick, I had things more important than romance to focus on. Getting her well, staying on the career track. I have things to do, Sebastian. I have responsibilities, and that affects having a partner too. I know we're married, but we're not financially linked. If we really moved in together, tried to start a life, that debt would affect us. Money rotted my parents' marriage, among other things. I still have a lot to pay off, and my mother only earns enough to look after her and my grandmother."

She let the sigh building in her chest loose. "It's why I get angry about the insurance companies. Harrison Health Care did a real number on my mother. It's why I hate that side of the job, how they feed on poor people and their families for greed. You have enough money not to struggle, and I won't for a long time because of rich men who sit in their skyscrapers pushing paper and misery around."

"Harrison Health Care? That's who you owe the debt to?" She saw his jaw clench, the twitch beneath his cheek.

She finally looked him in the eye. "Yes. They didn't cover the treatment fully, and the deductibles were huge. With that and my student debt, I'll be working another few years to get out from under it all. My mother helps, but she can't cover a lot of it, and I won't let her. I can't just start living a selfish life. I can't afford to want things for myself. Those two women sacrificed for years to raise me, help me become a doctor. I owe them everything, and when they needed me, I stepped up. I wanted to do it. I've taken everything on my shoulders for so long I don't know what it's like to not feel that weight.

"You are a stellar doctor, Sebastian, but you don't have family. It's just been me and them—forever. I can't risk anything that might jeopardize the life I want for them, for myself. I have to succeed, to give them the life they deserve, and prove that all their sacrifices were worth it. You distract me, Brown, in the best and worst ways, but I am terrified that one day we'll derail and knock everything off the track in our wake."

Sebastian didn't say anything for the longest time. He just sat there on the couch like a statue. Frozen, inert. Probably processing the fact that he had fallen for a woman who wasn't exactly a prospect to start a future with.

"I didn't know," he said eventually, his expression stony. "I wish you'd told me."

"I didn't tell anyone, really. Selina knows that money is tight, but I never told her about the whole thing. She offered me a cheap place to live, and if I'd told her she would probably have wanted to help more. I don't want that, from anyone. I don't need to be looked after. She's my mother, and I chose this career path. I just thought that you should know, because if we do this, really do this? It will affect you at some point, and I don't want you to resent me for it or try to ride in on a white horse and save me. It won't work, and we don't even know if we can be real. We've only ever been faking it, and we still have residencies to go through. That's more stress, more work. Over fifty percent of marriages end in divorce, Sebastian. I can't see us being one of the lucky ones, and I just can't take the risk."

He didn't reply, and she knew he was processing. Probably realizing the truth of what she was saying. Residency, especially as a cardiac surgical resident, was brutal. It was competitive and grueling, with no room for error or taking your eye off the ball. Surgeons were notoriously meticulous and driven. Those who did have families kept their lives separate for good reason. In the OR, there was no room for broken hearts or complications that didn't involve the patient on the operating table.

"How much do you owe?"

Of all the things he could have said, she didn't expect that question.

"Enough. I've been paying it for years. I will be for a few more yet."

"Because your mother's insurance wasn't covering everything. Even though you thought the premiums and coverage was enough."

The sadness in his voice took her by surprise. He sounded…deflated. Defeated.

"The policy was the best we could get. Her job doesn't come with medical, just dental. I didn't realize that there were so many loopholes. It's why I get angry at work, like when Hank died. His family lost him, but they will still have that debt to deal with. His insurance was for his care, not to pay off some corporation and line some CEO's pockets while they avoid footing the bill with some clever loopholes.

"I tried to appeal it for my mother at the time, took it to the top but they weren't interested. I didn't have the money to file some lawsuit I wasn't going to win. It was right there in the fine print, all the deductions and exemptions for different things. I don't want my mom to worry about it, so I hide most of it. When she was sick she gave me permission to be the point of contact. She doesn't even know how much it is. She pays a little each month, and I tell her I match it and it's covered, but I actually pay a lot more."

"So that's why you need to stay here. For the residency. It's not just to be close, it's for the expense too."

She felt lighter, telling him. It felt good to tell someone the whole truth. She'd been keeping it in so long, she didn't realize how much of a toll it had taken on her till she could voice it to another person. Someone she trusted to keep her secret.

"I'm sorry I didn't tell you, but other than at the hospital, my accounts aren't listed to this address. You won't be liable for any of the debt if the worst happens, because your name isn't mentioned."

"My name…" He shook his head, huffing out a deep sigh. "Taylor, my name is on it."

What? That wasn't true. She'd never listed him on one piece of paperwork. Other than their marriage certificate, the paperwork kept them separate.

"What do you mean, your name?" Her stomach dipped. "Did they write to you or something? That doesn't make sense—it's in my mother's name. I'm her appointee."

"My real name isn't Brown, Taylor. I took my mother's maiden name legally when I moved here. I wanted a fresh start. To be recognized for my own talent, not the legacy of someone else."

"Legacy?" Her brain must be on the fritz.

Having no clue what he was talking about, she pressed further. Made a joke of it, their old default when things got tense. "What are you? A Disney prince or something?"

He didn't laugh. Instead he took her hand in his. "My father is the CEO of Harrison Health Care. It's why I walked away from them all. I wasn't lying when I said we weren't close. I left them for good. Changed my name. I was born Sebastian Harrison, their sole heir."

"You're…their son?"

He dipped his head, his face bleak. "My dad always wanted me to take over, but I wanted to be a surgeon. So he agreed to let me get my doctorate. He figured that it would be an edge in business down the line, having a son who had a medical degree. But I saw things I didn't like." He cupped her jaw, rubbing his thumb along her cheek when a tear splashed free. "I saw people like Hank and your mother suffering while he just got richer. I couldn't do it, and I told him I was going to study to be a surgeon. That I wouldn't be following in good old Daddy's footsteps. I had some money that my grandfather left me, so I didn't need to rely on him to finish my studies."

"And he refused."

He smiled, a proud, sad tilt of the lips. "Yes, he decided to give me an ultimatum instead. Either I toed the family line, or I walked away. He wouldn't leave me anything, and I wasn't allowed to contact them again."

"Oh, Sebastian…" Her heart broke.

"It's okay. I got out. I got the offer to come to Vegas, and I got on that plane and never looked back. I planned to bury myself in work, being Dr. Brown, and then a fiery intern walked in the first day and royally rocked my world."

She laughed, a snotty, wet guffaw as she remembered that first day together.

"She sounds amazing."

His lips tilted at the corners. "She is, so much so that I married her. She's being tilting my axis ever since."

She felt so happy, so elated that they had shared their secrets. She didn't care what his last name was, or hers. She should care, hating Harrison Health Care as she did. But she knew him, his heart. He was nothing like that; he'd walked away because he felt as she did. He was here, and she cared about him. He hadn't run or tried to fix things for her. He'd listened while she spilled her guts and laid himself bare in return. He was strong, stubborn. His independence matched hers. Maybe, if they got their residencies together, stayed here, it would work. They could remain married and be happy. Then he spoke again, and her dreams popped like a balloon.

"Let me pay off that medical debt. I have the

money. My grandfather was the previous CEO. He made sure I was comfortable."

She wrenched away from him, off the couch. "Not a chance. Are you kidding?"

"Taylor, it's just money. You're my wife—"

"Just money?" She wanted to claw his tongue out for that. He hadn't listened to a word she'd said. He didn't want a partner, an equal, after all. Taking his money would mean that she owed him, and that was never going to happen. She'd rather sell an organ to a trafficker. "Just money? Wow! Spoken like a true nepo baby."

He reacted instantly, jumping off the couch and standing toe to toe with her now. "What's your problem? It's me! I don't expect anything from you. I never would. Just to make your life easier so you can concentrate on work is more than enough. I can help, I want to help. You can be free and live your life for yourself for once!"

"By paying my mother's bills like it's nothing? I promised myself a long time ago that I would never accept help from a man, would never rely on another person to get where I wanted in life. This isn't Narnia, it's the real world. Accepting a handout would go against everything I stand for. I don't want to owe anyone a damn thing, even you—and I don't need help! I would rather die!"

"Oh come on, it's not like that. I promise, I just meant it because I want to look after you.

I want to be in your life, make it easier. It's my money, not—"

"Exactly, it's your money!" she screamed back. "I don't want a penny of it, Sebastian." She wrenched the ring off her finger and threw it at him. "I don't want anything, come to think of it. We never knew each other, did we? I didn't tell you my life story, and you sure as hell didn't tell me yours. That was obviously for a reason. I should have trusted my gut, kept my distance. We hated each other! I should have known better! I knew that this was a bad idea. I'm leaving."

"Leaving? No, Taylor—"

He grabbed her arm as she strode to her bedroom. She yanked it back. "Don't touch me! It's over, Sebastian." He raised his hands in surrender, stepping back.

"I'm sorry. I would never hurt you. I just don't want you to leave. Where will you go? You live here, you belong here, with me."

"I belong to myself, and the fact that you don't get that is exactly why I need to leave." She looked around the lounge, at the medical books stacked on the side table, the comfy blanket on the back of the couch. Tears filled her eyes, but she had to get out of here. She felt so stupid, so out of her depth.

He thought he could just pay her debt off. Make it all better with money. They would never be equals, never be cut from the same cloth. She should have known better than to buy in to the fairy tale. Her mother and grandmother had never gotten it. They had ended up alone, regretting their relationship choices.

"I don't want to fake this anymore," she declared.

"Then don't!" Sebastian yelled, his hands coming up to touch her but stopping himself at the last minute. "Put your ring back on, and stay. Fight for me, for us. None of this changes anything. I'm falling for you, and I won't stop. I am not my father's son. I am not his mistakes. I want to be here, doing surgery—helping people. Just like you. I want to be in your life, protect you, make it better."

"By writing a check like some big shot?"

His face was stone now. "That was never me. I walked away from that fake life."

"And right into another one with me. Aren't you tired of pretending? Because I am done. Once the residencies are announced, we'll file for divorce. If we end up in the Valley together, we'll tell people we ended things amicably. Pressure of the job, whatever."

"I won't do that," he half growled. "It's not true."

She laughed, a hollow, bitter laugh that felt like it scooped the insides of her body out onto the floor.

"Since when has the truth been a problem for

us, hubby? I'll come back for my stuff next time you're out."

She heard him call her name but kept moving. Didn't stop till she was at Selina's front door. She vaguely remembered the cab ride. Watching Vegas through the car window and her tears.

Alone again. Isn't this what you wanted? She rubbed the skin of her bare finger, and burst into tears all over again.

CHAPTER FOURTEEN

In the days after the night she left Sebastian's flat, Taylor was on autopilot. She was living on grilled cheese, ice cream and the snacks in her locker, along with enough coffee to make Starbucks balk. She was in shock. A heavy, never-ending sense of dread that something was missing from her life. Like a purpose, or a limb.

She couldn't get her head around how things had changed. For instance, the fact that Patrick and Selina had been carrying on with each other for weeks. Earlier that morning, dragging herself out of her old bed, she'd gone into Selina's bedroom with a cup of coffee, only to be confronted by his naked bottom. He'd been sneaking into the apartment when she'd gone to sleep, and Selina had kept it from her.

"Peace offering, since you dropped the coffee you made this morning."

Taylor lifted her head from her desk in the intern lounge, taking the to-go cup with a raised brow.

"I hope your carpet never recovers. I know my

eyes won't—my retinas are still singed from seeing Patrick's naked ass."

Selina dropped into the chair next to her with a dreamy sigh, cradling her own cup to her chest. "Pretty nice, isn't it? I swear, those scrub trousers do him no favors. That is a work of art, and you should see the front."

Taylor almost choked on her latte. "Eww! Can you not? He's like my little brother."

Selina cackled. "Yeah, well, he's not mine. That man is fine." Each to their own. Selina was rather partial to a larger, far goofier intern. "Besides, it's just a bit of fun. Nothing that HR needs to know about."

"Oh yeah? Well, use a condom, and don't come to me when you wake up married." When Selina shot her a pity glance, she stuck her tongue out. "Sorry. I am happy for you, if it's what you want. You can tell him he doesn't have to sneak into the apartment anymore, and if he could wear pants at all times, even better."

"Will do. I'm sorry I didn't tell you, but you and Sebastian were having problems, and you were so preoccupied, I didn't want to bother you. Have you spoken to him yet?"

Selina clicked her pen. *Click click click.* It was a habit she'd developed the last few days, an annoying little quirk but at least it saved her fingers from permanent damage.

"No. I got my stuff when he was stuck in surgery. He's keeping his distance, which is for the best. I want him to treat me like everyone else." He was only speaking to her at work when he had to, and even then it was short and succinct. She was pretty sure that a few of the staff had picked up that something wasn't quite right, but they were professional enough to ignore it.

She just needed to get through today. The day that she'd been working toward. Dr. Ashanda was due to make the residency announcements today, and then she could relax. Everything would be back to normal. She would still live with Selina, who was sure to get her spot. She would keep paying the debt, and work hard. Look after her mother and grandmother. Enjoy the fact that everything was coming to fruition.

"I still think that all this can be sorted out. You told me he has feelings for you. I know for sure you are in love with him—"

Taylor opened her mouth to argue the point, but Selina shushed her with an accusing finger.

"You have been a wreck since you showed up back here. You're like some kind of AI bot at work—you never sleep. You live on caffeine and junk food, and the other night you cried when the hockey match was on. You love him, you stubborn idiot. I don't get why you just left him when you were so close to getting everything you wanted and more. He's perfect for you, and you know it."

"Who's perfect?"

Patrick thrust his head through the door of the intern lounge, startling them both.

"You are, darling," Selina laughed. "We were just discussing your rather lovely bottom. Taylor thinks it's not peachy, but I utterly disagree."

Patrick blushed, his entire face turning red, and he yanked the door open a little farther to reveal Sebastian standing behind him with a hug, scowl marring his features. He leaned in close, whispering to Pat in a gruff voice but Patrick shrugged him off.

"We can work in here—it's our lounge too." Another scowl came his way, which Patrick ignored as he practically pulled Sebastian into the office behind him. "Don't mind Dr. Brown here. I think he's just missing surgery. He's been like a bear with a sore head all week, come to think of it. Dr. Ashanda pulling us off rotation to catch up on research projects? I think she's going easy on us."

Taylor bit at her lip, watching Sebastian as he crossed the room to the desk farthest from all of them and started reading from a file he'd brought with him. Patrick nodded at Taylor, a speak-to-him move that made Taylor wince. There was no speaking to him. It was done. This was the new them. No fighting, no banter. No threatening to take scalpels to each other or dragging each other into storage rooms. Nope. None of that. Now it was a new game they were playing. Pretending the other didn't exist. She had to admit, it wasn't the best game that they'd played, but it was for the best, right?

Selina sighed, giving Taylor a pointed look. "Well, as long as we all get picked for residency here, I'll do whatever she says. Heck, I'd scrub the toilets if it meant getting my spot. Right, Tay? Seb?"

"Er…yeah," she mumbled. Sebastian glared her way, his expression so icy she shivered involuntarily.

"Sure," he sneered. "Nothing else matters, right, Cousins? As long as you get what you want."

"Sebastian, I—"

"Don't bother," he snapped, closing the file and shoving it down on the desk. "You know what I want to hear from you. Anything else doesn't concern me. You don't want me, now you know everything, right? I figured as much anyway. Should have stuck to my gut in the first place."

"Hey, man," Patrick admonished. "Take it easy. We're all friends, right?"

His snort was short and sharp. "Sure, Pat. Friends. Like Taylor and I were ever friends."

Taylor felt the sting of tears at the back of her eyes and willed them to go away with every fiber of her being. He was so hurt and angry, she couldn't bear it. Because she felt it too. Had been second-guessing herself since the minute she'd left him. But then she remembered how she'd felt when she'd found out who his father was. The fact that he'd offered her money that came from the backs of vulnerable, hardworking people like her mother just didn't sit right with her. The fact that he'd not taken note of her independence, or her need to do things on her own—in her own way. Without anyone's help. This wasn't a coffee or a hot chocolate—it meant owing another person.

She just couldn't do it, not even for him. It was just another reason that they couldn't be together. She couldn't afford to rely on someone like her mother and grandmother had before her. It didn't get them anywhere. If things got tough, would he still stick by her? He could walk out of his life and go back to his old one whenever he liked. He wasn't stuck by circumstance. If he hadn't been born a Harrison, if they hadn't started out like they had… The ifs were many and pointless.

"Patrick, let's go and get some lunch, huh? Bring some back to these two?" Selina suggested.

Patrick, ever observant, looked down at his watch with a frown. "Lunch? It's a bit early."

"Now, Patrick. I'll buy you a doughnut." She flashed him a devilish grin. "And owe you one later."

Patrick's tail practically wagged.

"Say less. Catch you later, bud."

When they were left alone, the tension in the air

intensified. She glanced Sebastian's way, but he was cold. She could see it in his face, the way his whole body was practically hugging the wall behind his desk. He didn't want to be here. Near her.

"Sebastian."

Nothing. He didn't even flinch.

"Sebastian."

"Cousins, I'm busy. Whatever you have to say, it can wait."

His phone lit up with a call, and for the first time, his eyes shifted to hers.

"I need to take this," he growled through a jaw clenched so tight she was surprised his teeth didn't crack in half. "In private."

Well, that was that then. Any hope that they could at least be amicable was lost. She couldn't blame him. She was hurt too, and the author of their misfortune.

"Fine." She left the room, sagging in the hallway outside as the weight of her decision truly hit home. *He hates me for real now. No more pretending on that score.* Their rivalry would be real now. If they both ended up staying in Vegas, this was what she'd have to look forward to. Him knowing all the real parts of her, everything they had been through, and despising her for it. They would have to work alongside each other, and then she'd go home to Selina and he'd probably move on. Find someone who wasn't so complicated. Someone who wasn't afraid to give him her whole heart and damn the consequences. She'd probably have money too, and no daddy issues that made her untrusting and barbed.

"Thank you, sir, I am looking forward to it."

His voice filtered over to her, and she tried not to listen. Who was he talking to? He sounded different, less cold. Perhaps that severe tone was reserved only for her from now on. The irony that this was the only thing of his she'd have to herself just about cut her heart in two.

"Family?" She heard his pause and wished she could see his face. See what he was thinking. Whether his brows were furrowed in that way of his. "Nope. I have no family—it will just be me… Yes… Okay… Thanks again. Speak to you soon."

No family. It was true, right? He didn't have any family to speak of. It didn't mean it didn't hurt to hear it. Who was he talking to anyway? Maybe he was planning his next date. There were plenty of nurses around here who would give their medical license for a chance to snag him. Maybe this was his way of moving on. Once the residencies were announced, they could announce their divorce, right? Everyone had seen how different they'd been around each other since their big fight. Their divorce would cause as much shock as their marriage announcement did, and Dr. Ashanda would probably be angry, but they'd have secured the residency spots. Then things would go back to normal. The scandal would be soon forgotten in the bustle of practicing medicine. Perhaps Selina and Patrick would make their new thing more than what they were implying it was, and then they would be the next people to visit HR.

She heard Sebastian's heavy exhale. Was he… bothered?

She needed to talk to him, to try to at least explain her reasoning. She'd been blindsided by his offer of money, and he needed to know that she wasn't rejecting him because of his father. It was more than that. It was everything. The whirlwind way they'd ended up married, the feelings that she'd never told him about. The Cousins women never got their happy-ever-after, did they, and they were fine. They'd survived. She'd been brought up to only rely on herself and no man. She was hardwired to be independent, and with him, she wasn't. She was needy, and distracted, and goofy.

He challenged her right out of her comfort zone, and if he left? If they really gave things a chance and it failed? It would wreck her. Havoc and chaos would take over, and she couldn't afford that, financially, mentally, emotionally. Sebastian Brown was the kind of man a woman didn't let go of. Except if you were her: battle-scarred, debt-ridden, terrified Taylor Cousins. The woman who everyone thought was a stellar surgeon but had a heart that was as protected as her patients'.

She took a step, and her beeper went off. Inside the room, she heard Sebastian's go off at the same time. When she heard him get up out of his chair, she ran down the corridor and hid around the corner. Checking the message, her broken heart skipped a beat. They were being summoned to the intern director's office. The residency decisions were about to be announced.

This is it, Taylor. Everything you've been working for.

Everything she'd sacrificed to get here would be worth it. Giving up Sebastian, playing along with the marriage, breaking her own heart for her goal. It was all going to pay off.

CHAPTER FIFTEEN

"THANK YOU FOR COMING," Dr. Ashanda addressed the room. Sebastian had come in last, slinking in and hanging in the back. When Taylor looked his way, he turned his head, focusing on a spot on the carpet. "I know you have all been working on your research projects, and eagerly anticipating the results of the residency decisions. As you know, we only have a few spots available in each department. Two from my own cardio department, along with one for OB and Maternity, two for Plastic Surgery and ENT, along with General Surgery, and a few other departments.

"I know that some of the other department heads have already chosen from other submissions, and some of you have already accepted spots elsewhere. Therefore, I will make this short. If I say your name, then your time here at the Valley is over. I wish you all the best in your future endeavors, and as you will all no doubt be eager to start your next steps, I am happy to dismiss you all for the day early. The new interns are in today, starting their orientations, so they will be working with the department heads."

With Selina and Patrick flanking Taylor on either side, the whole room held its breath. Each name was read out, and the interns filtered away. One of them, a terrible worker named Erin, burst into tears, screaming off down the corridor.

"This is brutal," Patrick muttered. "I swear, if I don't get picked I might sob myself."

"Suck it up," Selina muttered out of the corner of her mouth. "You have really turned things around."

Patrick looked at her, and Taylor could see the admiration written all over his face. "Thanks to you, my little study buddy."

"Get a room," Taylor hissed just as Dr. Ashanda spoke again.

"And for our first appointment at the Valley, Patrick Rowan."

"Yes!" Patrick punched the air, earning him a stern look from Dr. Ashanda that soon lost its heat.

"Yes," she smirked. "Congratulations, Dr. Rowan. It was a surprise to me too, but you have earned it. Go see your department head." She turned her gaze to Selina. "And take Selina and Josie with you, would you?" This time, that smirk turned into a real smile. "OB is waiting for their two new residents."

Selina squeaked, grabbing Taylor's hand so

hard and so fast her fingers made little cracking sounds. Patrick made a *woo-hoo* sound and covered it with a cough.

"Congratulations, both of you," Taylor said. She was so happy for them both. They were staying together, and she had a feeling that Patrick was going to be more of a fixture around their apartment over the coming months. "Proud of you."

Selina hugged her tight, Patrick enveloping them both in a big dopey cuddle until Dr. Ashanda made a none-too-subtle point of clearing her throat.

"Good luck!" Selina mouthed, and then the three of them were out of the door. As she watched them leave, Taylor saw that it was just her and Sebastian. They were the last ones standing. He stepped forward, taking Patrick's place next to her but leaving a large gap between them. Dr. Ashanda eyed them both, her eyes taking in their awkward stances. Her eyes narrowed.

"I apologize for leaving the two of you till last, but I wanted to take the time to impress upon you how well I think you have handled yourselves during this...situation."

That didn't sound good. In fact, it sounded like she was being nice before pulling the rip cord and shoving them both out of the plane. Taylor couldn't breathe. It was taking everything she said to stay standing. She'd not applied anywhere else. She only wanted Vegas. If she lost the position now, what would be left for her? She'd be a divorcée, unemployed and broke. Her mother and grandmother would struggle to keep the house. She…couldn't pull enough air into her lungs.

"Breathe," Sebastian said. Low enough that she barely heard him, but it helped. She felt steadier, like he knew what she was thinking and was telling her it was going to be okay.

Dr. Ashanda reached over her desk and pulled out two sealed envelopes. "Here are your offers, for my department. I would be delighted to have you both at the Valley as my cardiac residents. I appreciate that living and working together, along with managing the scrutiny of your colleagues, might have been difficult, but you have both received nothing but glowing recommendations from not only the other department heads, but your patients as well. Just let me know by the end of the week. Take the rest of the day, tomorrow, and get some rest. The research projects will still be there tomorrow, and next week we can start discussing your new duties."

She rolled her eyes. Actually, honest to god rolled her eyes. "Which will include helping to whip the new interns into shape. One of them hacked a hole into one of the model hearts today in the practice lab. I genuinely fear for the future of medicine sometimes."

Taylor's head was spinning again. "So, we got the spots?"

"Did I not just say that?"

"Er…yes! Yes, thank you! I—we—won't let you down." Realizing that he hadn't said a word, she glanced at him. "Right, Sebastian?"

He was staring down at the packet in his hands, his expression utterly at odds to what she expected. He wanted this, right? He wanted this residency just as much as she did. He had a home here, friends. Was it because of her? The thought of having to keep up the pretense while the divorce came through and they could just be colleagues again?

Looking at the packet in his hand one more time, he straightened his shoulders and held it out to Dr. Ashanda.

"I'm sorry. I am beyond grateful for the opportunity, but Boston General actually made me an offer. I applied a while ago, earlier in the internship. I'm due to fly out in two days to meet with their head of cardio."

It was the first time she'd seen Dr. Ashanda shocked. *You and me both, sister.*

"I see. I thought that, as you and Dr. Cousins are married now, you would be continuing on with us. You two were always my best candidates, but if it's too much—"

"It's not," Sebastian cut in. "Taylor and I always put our careers first. Right, Dr. Cousins?"

She could barely lift her head long enough to nod. She couldn't even look at him. He hated her so much that he didn't even want to be in the same state.

"Right," she managed to get out, her voice cracking.

Dr. Ashanda's gaze flicked between the two of them, and whatever she saw there made her lips purse. "Well, I can hold the spot till Monday. After that I will have to give it to my third choice." She pushed the packet back his way. "Consider your options. Go to Boston, of course, but remember that there is a lot for you here in Vegas." She turned back to Taylor, and there was an unmistakable tinge of pity in her expression. "Congratulations, Doctors. You have a lot to be proud of."

Taylor had to speak to him. She had to make this right. Apologize, ask him to think about staying. She'd already reconciled herself to the divorce, but never seeing him again? Unthinkable. Even if he spent his time hating her, she would prefer that to him leaving for Boston and not being in her life at all.

When he turned to leave, the packet clutched in his tight fist, she went to follow him, but fate, as always, was a cruel mistress.

"Dr. Cousins, hang back a moment. I need to discuss something with you."

No, no, no! Not now.

"I…er…need a minute with Sebastian first, if that's okay?"

"That's okay, wifey." His tone was a little less cold, but it still held no real warmth. "Take your time."

He dashed out of the office as if it was on fire, leaving her standing there feeling like he'd slapped her in the face. When she turned back, Dr. Ashanda motioned her toward the nearest chair.

"I'm sorry to keep you, but I thought you might like to know. I had Hank's family come in earlier, to thank us for our care."

"Oh." She smiled, feeling empty inside. "That's really nice."

"Yes, and I know that you were upset for the family when we lost him, but they informed me that someone stepped in and paid the bill in full."

"What? The whole thing? Who would…?"

Dr. Ashanda took the seat next to her. "The benefactor chose to remain anonymous, but I have a theory. I think you might have an idea yourself. This is confidential, of course."

Sebastian. Sebastian had paid their whole bill? He knew how upset she was about it; they'd argued about it. He'd used his family money to help them, and the family would never know it was one of Hank's doctors.

"I don't miss much around here, Dr. Cousins. I see all, and I know that you are conflicted right now. I must admit, Dr. Brown's decision was a shock to me too."

"I didn't know," she admitted, the reality of Sebastian leaving for a new life hitting her all over again. "Things haven't been easy between us."

"I know that too."

"You do?" Oh, right. They hadn't exactly been love's young dream lately.

"I told you, I see everything. Heart surgery is difficult. It's stressful, and only the best of the best can have a damaged but beating heart in front of them and make it better. Life is like that too. I'm sure that whatever is going on between you, it can be resolved."

"I appreciate your faith, but I'm not so sure."

Dr. Ashanda patted the packet in her hands. "This is your future, Taylor. You've worked hard to get here. Just remember that work isn't everything. I had a man like Dr. Brown once." She looked almost wistful as her gaze turned to the many awards adorning the walls. "I chose the medicine, and I didn't fight hard enough to have more. I'm happy with my life, but when the operating lights go out and I leave the hospital, I'm alone." She turned back to Taylor and grinned. "Besides, Boston sucks. The head cardio surgeon there is a buffoon."

CHAPTER SIXTEEN

GRAMS SNATCHED THE biscuit barrel off Taylor's lap, tutting as she took in her couch potato state.

"Cookies for breakfast? Really?"

Taylor nibbled the one she had in her hand, wincing as she took in all the crumbs and chocolate smears on her pyjamas.

"Yep. I needed a sugar hit."

"You need a shower and a kick up the behind," Grams retorted, looking at Sandra with a determined look on her face. "You know, we did this."

"Did what?"

After the meeting with Dr. Ashanda, Taylor had looked for Sebastian, but not one person had seen him. When she ran out to the car park, his car was gone. His phone was turned off. He'd dropped off the face of the earth. She could have gone to his apartment, but Patrick said he wasn't there. Sebastian had told him that he was going away and didn't want to be contacted.

"Those were his exact words, Tay. I'm sorry," Patrick said. He and Selina were as shocked as she was to hear about Boston. Patrick, especially. It was safe to say that their golden retriever friend was feeling more than a little distraught at the possible loss of his best friend and colleague. When they all tramped back to Selina's and saw the divorce papers on the mat, Taylor had left. Turned up at her mother's house full of tears and still clutching the damn papers. God knows what he'd done to get the papers so fast, but it was official. Happening. He'd signed his name, and she'd never hated seeing his signature so much in her entire life.

She barely registered the look of confusion her mother was showing Grams, but her grandmother was a determined woman.

"We did this to her. Made her too independent, too damn mistrustful of people."

"Mom," Sandra sighed. "We raised her to be strong. What's wrong with that?"

Grams tutted and came to sit next to Taylor, ripping the cookie right out of her hand.

"Taylor Leigh Cousins, I don't say this to you lightly. I have never been anything but proud of you. Since the day you were born, you were curious about the world. Fearless. While the other kids played, you had your head in a book. You once took the television apart, just to see how the parts all fit together."

Taylor smiled at the memory. It had taken her hours to take it apart, and then she thought her mother was going to go mental when she couldn't put it back together. It was just something she wanted to do. It had been on the fritz for a while, and with the financial pressures, she'd been desperate to help her family.

"I remember that."

"And we were both so mad at first, but you did it. You fixed it." She pursed her lips, and for the first time in a long time, she looked every inch her age. Her whole body seemed to deflate in the chair. "You've always fixed things for us, and that's not your job."

"Grams, I—"

"Grams nothing. I know that you're paying more for the insurance bills than you let on."

Taylor's heart stuttered in her chest. "How?" She looked at her mother, who didn't look the least surprised, or happy.

"We're Cousins women, honey. We don't miss anything, but we couldn't help. You wouldn't have let us, even if we could. You take on so much, worry so much, you forgot to have your own life. Till Sebastian. We knew the second you brought him home that your relationship was real, and he was the one for you."

"It was fake," she started to say, but it fell flat. "In the beginning, anyway. But what does it matter now? He's leaving—you saw the papers. He wants out. I'm fine on my own, anyway. Relying on someone else just leads to trouble."

Sandra took a seat on her other side. "Having someone you love is more than that, darling. Not every story ends badly. Letting someone take care of you isn't a weakness."

"So why did it feel like that when he offered the money? Did you not listen to what I told you last night?"

"You mean when you turned up here, broken and crying? I heard everything, but he paid for that patient's treatment costs, helped that family and never took an ounce of credit. His grandfather sounds like a good man. That money might come from people suffering, but you tell me which money doesn't. We live in Vegas, sweetheart. All those fancy fountains and lights are paid for by the misery and suffering of other people. People just trying to live life on their own terms, just like Sebastian is now. He walked away from his whole life, made his own. He helps save people, just like you. When he offered you that money, it was to make your life easier. He wanted to help the woman he loves, and you threw it in his face. What if your mother and I had done that to you, when you stepped in? Sometimes, it's okay to need someone, honey. It won't make you any less of the strong woman you are."

Sebastian's crestfallen face popped right into her head. She'd been so nasty to him, so unwilling to talk. To try. Since they got together, he'd helped her. He'd saved her from that patient, defended her. Cared for her. Bought things to make his home feel a little more like hers, too. Held her in the night, supported her dreams. Even when they were enemies, he'd made her a better doctor. He'd kept her fighting even when she felt low and defeated and wanted to give up. He'd even come here, had dinner with her family and been nothing but nice.

Sure, he was a Harrison, but he never felt like one. He was always Sebestian Brown to her, and she could see why he'd kept things from her. Why he didn't want his past to color his future. She'd kept things from him too, about her family and their struggles. Hell, she'd even told him how much she hated his family's company, but he had come clean, hadn't he? He'd told the truth, even though he knew it might hurt her.

"I really did, didn't I?" She sat up, feeling panicked. "He was trying to be with me, and I pushed him away. All the way to Boston. Once he gets there, he'll leave. I know it. They will offer him the spot, and I won't see him again. He wanted this too, Vegas. The Valley. I know he did, he wanted to stay." The tears were falling now as she replayed everything in her head, minus the stubborn filter she'd been running it all through. "I really messed things up, didn't I? Mom? Grams?"

"Yes," they both said in unison. Her mother laughed, hugging her close. "But what we women in this family do best is making the best of a bad situation."

Grams reached for Taylor's phone, jabbing a few buttons.

"How do you work this thing? Where's the internet button?"

Taylor reached for it, bemused at the change in conversation. What was Grams looking for, a new recipe?

"Give it here. What are you trying to do?"

Grams shoved it into her hands. "Flight information. Sandra, get your keys. We're going on a road trip."

"What? No, I can't. I... I... I'm not even dressed." Grams wasn't listening; she was already grabbing her shoes, handbag on her arm. "Mom, I can't just turn up at the airport. He doesn't want me. He served me the divorce papers, remember?"

Her mother grabbed the phone from her, tapping a few keys and holding the screen aloft.

"There are two flights to Boston today. One leaves in an hour. It's decision time, darling. Do you want to fight for what you want, or give up? Because Mamma didn't raise no quitter."

She looked at the screen. Fifty-six minutes. She might have as little as fifty-six minutes, and then her husband would be leaving the state, and her life, forever. She could just carry on. Let him go. She could eat all the cookies in the house and cry watching *The Notebook*. She could stay in Vegas with Selina and Patrick. Live the life that a month ago was all she wanted. Or she could get dressed, pull her big-girl panties up and go beg the man she loved to make a life with her.

"Well?" Grams shrieked. "What are we doing? Are we going or not? Time's a-wasting!"

Taylor got to her feet, brushing off not only the cookie crumbs, but also her fear.

"Let's go get him," she laughed. "Get the car running!"

CHAPTER SEVENTEEN

A Tesla furiously honked as their car sped past.

"Sorry!" Taylor winced, hoping to god that a cop car wasn't nearby. Getting a ticket now would not be ideal. Her grandmother would probably put the cop in a headlock so they could escape. Ever since they'd got in the car she'd turned into some kind of speed-loving daredevil, and her mother wasn't much better.

"Put your foot down, Tay! You're not driving Miss Daisy!"

"My foot's down, Mom! The traffic's heavy."

"I told you we should have gotten her that blue light thingamajig for her birthday," her grandmother muttered from the back seat. She was sitting forward with both hands on the backs of the front seats, as if her leaning in would propel the car faster. "We could have smoked these clowns and been there by now."

"Smoked what?" her mother asked, her face a picture of confusion.

"We'll get there, okay? Without a police escort,

with a bit of luck. Anyway, those siren things are illegal, Grams. I told you."

"Illegal, shmegal. You're a doctor! You have emergencies all the time! You could tell them you're saving a broken heart! It's not exactly a lie, is it?" She tapped her daughter on the shoulder with a bony finger. "Sandra, stick your head out of the window and be a siren."

"Mom, I'm not doing that! Be serious!" Sandra protested.

"I am being serious! She's about to lose her husband, Sandy! If he gets on that plane, it's over! Do you know what that means? All the cookie dough in the world won't be enough, and if I have to sit through *The Notebook* again, I will sign myself into a retirement community in Miami and wait for the gators to get me! We need Sebastian back. He's family, and you don't just let good people walk out of it without a damn good ruckus to keep them!"

Taylor met her mother's eye, and the pair of them glanced back at Grams. All three women were acknowledging the seriousness of the moment. It wasn't just Taylor that loved Sebastian. It was all of them. He'd charmed them all, in his own way. They wanted him to stay, to be one of them. Taylor could see it now. The family dinners, the Christmases. All of the milestones they'd go through together. Anniversaries, children one day. Grams would love to be a great-grandmother. They would both spoil their children rotten.

They would all be worse off without him, and it wasn't about the money, or anything material. Sebastian was one of them now.

Taylor smiled at her family, tightening her grip on the wheel.

"Hang on tight," she warned and grinned. "Grams, keep an eye out for sirens."

Grams, whooped, and Sandra wound down her window and shouted to the other cars to move aside as Taylor pushed her foot down on the gas and wove through the traffic like Lewis Hamilton on a packed racetrack.

"That's more like it!" Grams shouted from the back, gripping the seats a little tighter as the airport came into view. They flew down the off ramp like a plane coming in to land, Sandra's old car juddering from the exertion.

The second they found a place to pull the car over, Taylor was out and running, her mother and grandmother cheering her on as they stayed to deal with the car and the very annoyed parking attendant who was heading over to them with a stern look on his face. Even in her panicked dash to get to Sebastian, she couldn't help but chuckle. That guy was *not* going to win. They were going to fold him like origami if he so much as raised his voice.

Departures was busy, filled with the usual suspects. Drained-looking tourists, most of them appearing more than a little worse for wear, ambled about with their souvenirs and suitcases, waiting for various check-ins. She wove through the crowds, heading straight for the information board. *Damn it.* The next flight was on time, and there was a last call for boarding. Yanking out her phone, she tried his number, but it went straight to voicemail. *Is he already on the plane?*

"No, no, no!" she wailed, trying it again in desperation. Voicemail again. "Come on! Don't do this to me!"

The check-in desk was still dealing with some of the passengers from his flight, and she desperately scanned every person for a glimpse of him. Nothing. He wasn't there. Had he gotten an earlier flight? The sense of gnawing, all-consuming dread in the pit of her stomach made her feel sick. She'd done this. She'd pushed him away. He'd spilled his guts to her, and she'd rejected him so badly he'd boarded a plane just to get away from her. She watched as the last passenger checked his bags, and the attendant closed the desk.

She could get a ticket. She could buy a ticket, get on the plane and stop him that way. People did it all the time, right? All of the movies did it. The lovesick character who paid exorbitant amounts of money to buy some obscure flight just to get through the gate. She could make it. She could be one of those ridiculous saps who held up the plane and poured out their feelings to the one who was trying to get away, right?

They'd got married in Vegas without having even kissed each other. Their marriage, their whole relationship, had been built on a rash decision. That was her and Sebastian, one big, impetuous, passionate storm. For a woman who had spent so long trying to control everything, to never let anyone derail her from reaching her goals and ruling out anything and everything else, she was lost. A goner for Sebastian Brown, and the life she'd built was emptier without him. Everything that she'd achieved was nothing without her husband by her side. She was going to do it. She was going to race to him, and not leave this damn airport without him by her side.

Reaching for her bag, she stilled. "Oh god, no." Tears filled her eyes and spilled over. Because her bag wasn't there. She'd run straight from the car and had only grabbed her phone. Her handbag was still sitting in the trunk of her car. She didn't have her passport, or even enough money without her credit card to buy an airport pretzel, let alone a plane ticket. Sinking to her knees, she ignored the curious stares of the strangers around her and instead, she stared at her phone screen.

The snap from their wedding day showed two smiling people, obviously a little merry from the twinkle in their eyes, holding each other. She'd vaguely remembered it at the time, a snapshot of the first moment of their married life captured by a grinning Elvis impersonator. They'd both separately set it as their screen savers, a funny little quirk that she'd thought nothing of at the time. Part of their ruse, their cover story for their colleagues and friends. Now all she could think about was what was on Sebastian's phone right now. Was their picture still there? How long into his new life would he wait to change it to something else? Some*one* else?

A fresh wave of sadness hit her, and as she wiped ineffectually at her tears, a shadow appeared from behind.

"Cousins?" Whirling around on bended knees, she almost landed on her butt, but he grabbed her shoulders, steadying her. "What are you doing here?"

"It's garbage day. You forgot to put the trash cans out."

His eyes searched hers, finally crinkling at the corners as he fought against his smile.

"Right. So you came here to chew me out?"

She shrugged, grateful that he was playing along. Seeing him standing there, his carry-on bag over his shoulder, she needed a minute. "Well, it was your turn. Just because you're moving across the country doesn't mean that you get out of chores."

He didn't fight the smirk on his face as he pulled her to her feet, his arm wrapping around her as if he was as scared as she was to let the other go.

"Noted. I think I might need a punishment, you know, for shirking off. You got one in mind?"

She pretended to think, her heart soaring both at his touch and their easy to-and-fro. This was them at their core, teasing and tender. She couldn't not have this in her life, not now. Annoying the hell out of Sebastian Brown was as exciting and as necessary to her as breathing in, as surgery used to be. Now it wasn't just her job that had her heart and soul.

"Well, you'll just have to come home. Make it right." She rested her hands on his chest, wanting to feel his heart beating. He covered them with his free hand, pushing them closer to his skin like he knew just what she was doing.

"I'm pretty sure we missed our chance, baby." Her own heart stopped, till he added, "The garbage men will already have been by. I'll have to do something else to make it up to you."

"You can bet your stethoscope you will. This is not the 1950s, bucko. Equal partners all the way."

He smiled, but it didn't reach his eyes.

"What are you really doing here, Taylor? Nothing's changed, has it?"

"It has. I was so hurt when you offered me that money, but I know why you did that now. Because you care. Because we are equal partners, and value each other's lives—outside of us. I get it now. I don't want to work without you either. We know each other, inside and out. It's how I know when I rejected you, it brought up your stuff too. Because you think no one could want the real you, and you're wrong on all counts. I know everything, and I am here, wanting you. Begging you not to run from *me* this time. I don't want to do any of this without you, Sebastian."

He raised a brow, pulling her closer. His eyes were wet with unshed tears.

"I'm trying to convince you not to get on that plane," she pressed.

He shook his head. "My plane left five minutes ago, Cousins."

"So you're staying? Really?"

It was his turn to shrug now, and she loved him for it.

"I just couldn't do it. I got to the gate, and everything in me told me to turn around. I don't want Boston, but I don't know how we can do this, after everything. How we trust each other without wrecking this when stuff comes up."

"Well, it's not been the greatest start to a marriage, granted."

"I never wanted to lie to you, Taylor. I never wanted that. The one thing about us was that we always held each other accountable, we pushed each other to be better people, even with all the sniping and bickering. Fighting with you was the best time of my life, wifey."

The tears were streaming down her face now, and he dipped to kiss them in turn. "You never treated me like Harrison Junior, and I loved being Sebastian Brown. I wanted to be the type of man who repaired some of the damage my family caused. Each life I saved was another step out of his shadow, but I was going to tell you. When we figured out what we were to each other, I was so happy."

"And then I told you about my mom."

He nodded, lifting both hands to her face and wiping the rest of the salty tears away. "I couldn't tell you then. You would never have looked at me that way again. I didn't want to lose you, but I still lied. I did it because I was scared, but I hated every second of it. I was terrified you would reject me like my family did. We have such baggage from our father figures, and we just didn't realize it. I was wrong for offering the money—I know. I knew you were independent, so I don't know why I said it. I just feel this need to be the man who's by your side, strong and certain. I am a better man because of you, and I want to do this, as partners who let each in. I want no more secrets, no more unspoken truths."

"Even about my cooking?"

They laughed together then, standing there in the busy airport like they were the only two people in the world.

"Don't push it," he murmured into the corner

of her mouth. "Your cooking is enough to put people *in* the hospital."

"Hey!" She went to swat at him, but he pinned her arms to him and dropped his mouth to hers. She melted into him the second their lips touched, grabbing at his jacket to pull him closer still. "I missed you, Brown," she breathed when they finally, reluctantly parted. "I know I messed up. I panicked, and I didn't think, which is sort of my MO if you haven't noticed. I lash out or double down on my default I-don't-need anyone persona when things get real. Don't go to Boston. Stay here. Take the residency."

"You mean it?" He looked so utterly hopeful and fearful—all at the same time—and it made her heart damn near explode. "You want me to stay? Work with you?"

"Well, I don't think there are many quickie wedding chapels in Boston, but I don't fancy risking the chance that my husband might take another wife on a whim."

His gorgeous eyes sparkled, his whole face dropping into a dreamy grin. "One wife is enough for any lifetime, trust me." His expression grew troubled once more. "And if I come back, what about us? What would we be to each other? Colleagues? Ex-spouses?" He looked so torn, so regretful it broke her heart all over again. Once upon a time, she lived to torture this man. Now she would burn the world down if it meant never having to see that look on his face ever again in her lifetime. "I signed the papers, remember? I… I thought that was what you wanted, after everything we—"

She pushed her index finger against his lips, silencing him.

"You signed the papers, but I didn't." His eyes bulged, a small smile threatening to pry apart his lips. "In fact, they might have suffered a little accident."

"Accident, eh? What did you do, try to cook them?"

"Hey! I can go right back home, you know! You can still catch the next flight to Boston."

"Not a chance," he laughed. "I am going to rib you about this very romantic gesture for the rest of our lives, trust me. Every time I leave a towel on the bathroom floor or a dish in the sink, this is going to be my get-out-of-trouble-scot-free card." Sticking his lips out in an exaggerated pout, he pulled her closer. "Sorry, wifey, for not cleaning up, but you did dash to the airport to bring me home." He put his lips back to normal to steal a kiss. "Sorry I didn't put down the toilet seat, but you declared your love for me in front of a crowd of people." Another kiss, this one a little longer, a touch more lustful. "See? I win. You can't live without me."

"Debatable," she smiled. "I was doing just fine before you came into my life."

"You were just waiting for me, baby. Admit it, life is a lot more fun with me around."

"Well, my blood pressure has certainly been different."

He kissed her again, pulling her ever tighter to him.

"Wait till I get you alone," he smirked. "I'll raise it and then some."

"Ooh," she teased. "Can't wait for that, hubby."

His eyes sparked at her words. "You love me, Taylor Cousins Brown, and that cannot be taken back. Now that you have me, it's for life. We do this, all out. For real, forever. No more secrets, no more letting our family drama keep us from loving each other. Being a doctor is important, but being with you, being your husband, that's what makes me happy."

"You're sure," she queried, feeling like it just couldn't be true. All the way over here, she was so focused on getting there before his plane left, she hadn't thought about his answer. The fact that he was so glad to see her was a relief, but her overthinking brain was still being a killjoy. "Because residencies are going to be horrendous, and we will probably still fight over every surgery, and disagree about treatment—"

"Brown," he chided, pushing his hand over her mouth to silence her. "That's half the reason we fell in love in the first place. I say bring it on."

Tucking her under his arm, he picked up his baggage and headed toward the doors.

"I know it was you that helped Hank's family." His step faltered for a second, but he kept walking. "Dr. Ashanda told me. That you used your money to help him, and didn't want to take any credit for it. I'm sorry for being so horrible to you about your offer. I don't want you to think that's what I came for either."

He whirled her to face him. "I get why you reacted the way you did. I considered giving the money away myself, more than once, but my grandfather was a good man. He cared about the people he did business with. My father only ever saw figures on a spreadsheet, risk against return. The way I see it, I only use that money when I need it. It helped me be free. I can right the balance by being there for my patients. Once residency is over, I can do pro bono work too. We both could. There's a world of people out there with no safety net at all. No insurance when they get sick. Between us, we could really make a difference. Selina and Patrick too."

She'd never thought of it that way. With their skills and positions, they really could do more than just save their patients. They could help them to avoid being ruined financially too.

"I think Selina would love that."

"Patrick will probably make a joke about free butt lifts, but I'm sure he would too. He's an idiot, but his heart is as big as his mouth." He chuckled as they started walking again. "In fact, we owe him big time. If he hadn't spillled the beans, we would never have given this marriage a go."

"Oh god," Taylor moaned. "He's going to be godfather to our babies, isn't he?"

She'd said it as a joke, but Sebastian dropped his bags and picked her off the floor.

"Babies? Are you trying to kill me? I have to be the luckiest man on the planet, Cousins Brown. You keep saying things like that, and I will consummate this marriage all over again right here, right now."

"Calm down, stud muffin. There's plenty of time for all that."

Rubbing his nose against hers as he held her to him, he rested his forehead against hers. That adorable grin of his was lighting his whole face up.

"I can't wait, wifey. Let's go home. I have phone calls to make, and then we are going to bed for the rest of the day." When she kissed him again, he spoke out of the side of his mouth. "Make that the week. Who needs a job? Screw the calls. I'll be a househusband. You suck at cooking anyway—it's perfect."

"Er..." Taylor pulled a face, nodding to the doors. "Hold that thought. I...sort of brought company." She turned Sebastian around and her mother and grandmother stood there, waving frantically. "I think they want to keep you too."

They ran forward, and Sebastian was ripped from her grasp and showered with hugs from the two women, who both talked at once.

"You're staying then?" Grams said when they finally let him go long enough to walk to the car. "For good?"

"I'm aiming to be wherever my wife is." He smiled, taking Taylor's hand in his. "Vegas is looking pretty good right about now."

Sandra wiped at a tear on her cheek. "Good, because you're family, Sebastian."

"Family," he murmured, his voice with emotion. "Yeah. A lot to stick around for."

"Thank the lord," Grams chimed in, looking positively spritely. "Saves me from baking so many cookies."

Taylor blushed, and all three women cracked out laughing. Sebastian looked at all three of them, an expression of bemusement on his handsome face.

"I'm going to have my work cut out for me with you three, aren't I?" A look of realization flashed across his features, and he dug into his pocket. "Oh, I have something for you, Taylor. I almost forgot."

Out of his pocket, he pulled out a ring. *Her ring.*

"You had that with you this whole time?"

"Of course I did," he murmured, lifting her hand and placing the ring back where it belonged.

"I had to keep you close to me somehow." He kissed the gold band. "Looks better where it is though." He turned to the rest of his family and picked up his bag. "Ladies, I'll drive."

Sandra let out a sigh. "As long as I don't have to be a siren, I'm in."

When Sebastian raised a brow, Taylor shrugged. "I'll tell you later. And if a cop pulls you over, don't be surprised if there's a very ticked off parking attendant tied up in the trunk."

EPILOGUE

Dr. Ashanda was in top form again. Her mood was always what could be described as "on edge" when it came to the day the new interns arrived after having completed their orientation. The four new residents loitered near the locker room, all dressed in their brandnew scrubs.

"Seen the puppies yet?" Patrick asked, mouth half full of bagel. Selina rolled her eyes, wiping a blob of cream cheese from his chin.

"Puppies?" Sebastian asked, leaning in to drop a quick kiss on Taylor's cheek, lowering her voice to whisper in her ear. "I missed you in bed this morning. Our next day off, I'm not letting you out of it."

"Yeah," an oblivious Patrick said in between mouthfuls. "You know, puppies. Young, eager little interns that still need to cut their teeth."

"I can't believe that we were ever like that." Selina smiled. "It feels like a long time ago. We really were clueless compared to now, weren't we?"

A flustered young woman came running up to

the locker room doors. When she saw the four of them standing there, she skidded to a halt. "I'm so sorry I'm late. I got into something in the car park. Some jackass cut me off, and…" She clocked the color of their scrubs and her rosy cheeks paled. "Sorry. I am never late, usually. I was top of my class in Boston, and this really, really won't happen again."

Sebastian motioned to the locker room doors, his face serious. "See that it doesn't. Dr. Ashanda is a stickler for punctuality, and believe me, you want to stay on her good side."

"Thank you, it won't. It's just…been a morning. I'm Ashley, by the way. I…"

The poor, flustered intern was about to walk through the door when she spotted a man striding her way. A handsome man who looked decidedly annoyed. "I don't believe it." Her expression escalated from stressed to murderous. "Excuse me. I have a jackass to talk to. You!" she bellowed, stomping over to the disgruntled man, her backpack swinging off one arm. The guy stopped as she confronted him, looking more than a little disturbed to see her. "Where did you get your driving license, clown college? You totally cut me off for that space and you know it!"

"I did?" He pulled at his hair, his face turning red. "Was your name on it? Did I miss it printed on the asphalt? You don't own the space, Miss

Magoo! I was already indicating for the spot. What do you think I was there for, my health?"

She popped her hip, stepping closer with her fists clenching by her sides.

"Never a good sign, when a woman changes her stance like that," Selina whispered.

"Good to know," Patrick whispered back. "Remind me to buy you flowers on the way home."

Ashley's huff was full of indignation. "Well, this is a hospital. Maybe you came to get a brain scan, you know—to see if you have one rattling around in that big fat head of yours!" The four of them watched aghast as the pair of the interns bickered all the way to the locker room door. When the warring duo both reached for the door at the same time, Taylor turned to Sebastian and saw he was already grinning.

"Why are you going in there?" the guy asked, looking like he wanted to make the woman disappear. "Oh my god, don't tell me. You're an—"

"Intern," she finished for him. "You have got to be kidding me. You're starting here today too?"

"Yep," he huffed. "Maybe you can come with me for the scan, get your eyes checked. And next time, I'm ramming you for the parking space, Ponytail."

He flicked the mane of blond hair that was hanging from a tight ponytail down her back, and she reacted like she'd been shot.

"Ram me? Ohh-ho-ho. Bring it on. I am going to make you rue the day you messed with me!"

They both got stuck smushed against each other going through the doors, which resulted in more insults and pushing and shoving till the pair fell through the opening, which closed behind them. For a moment, the four residents stood in the now relatively silent corridor processing what they had just witnessed.

"Is it me," Selina asked, "or do they remind you of someone?"

Sebastian laughed, pulling Taylor into his chest and hugging her tight.

"Nope," they both answered in unison.

"I don't know what you're talking about," Taylor giggled.

"Totally different," Sebastian added. "Still, if the interns have a night out in Vegas, we might need to prepare HR."

Patrick, having finished his bagel, chuckled to himself. "I think we're in for a hell of a year, guys."

Sebastian and Taylor looked at each other, marveling at the turn of events that had led them to today. They were all official residents in their chosen fields, here at the Valley. Married life was everything they never expected, and they were loving every minute. Working alongside each other in the cardio department, living together in his apartment, which was now filled with photos of them. Sebastian had blown their wedding photo up and it now took pride of place in their sitting room.

"Those two are going to be a nightmare to teach. Did you see the way they were looking at each other?" Patrick said.

Selina flicked him on the forehead. "Hey!" He moaned, rubbing the spot. "Not the face, Lina! It's my best feature!"

"Come on," she laughed, linking arms with him as they walked down the corridor together. "We have work to do. Catch you later, lovebirds."

Alone in the corridor, Sebastian sneaked a kiss.

"Dr. Brown! Not at work. I am a professional, unlike some."

"Sorry, Dr. Cousins Brown," he smirked, looking anything but. "I was just feeling a little nostalgic." He tilted his head to the locker room, where the arguing interns could still be heard bickering and banging lockers. "Reminds me of how we started."

"Oh yes, threats of violence and one-upmanship. Very Romeo and Juliet."

"I totally would have climbed up to your window if you'd given me the nod." There was a loud crash from the locker room, and they both winced. "Looks like we will have to keep a close eye on those two. I hope they don't worship the same speciality. There might be actual appendages lost."

"Ah well, at least they can sew each other up. Be good practice."

"I love you." He smiled. "I'm glad we're here together."

"Me too." She grinned back. "I love you too, Sebastian Brown." She leaned in close, and whispering into his ear, she breathed in a sultry voice. "Dr. Ashanda wants a resident on her triple bypass today, so I'll race you to the skills lab. Loser had to do the laundry."

She turned on her heel, racing down the corridor. Seb was hot on her heels, laughing as she sped away. "Bring it on, Granny Pants," he teased as they both dashed to the lab.

"Loser washes what?" she trilled back, feeling the fire ignite in her belly. Fueling her feet as she left her husband to choke on her dust. Life was great when you gave up control; she knew that now. That night in Vegas had changed everything, for the better. Now she had a husband who challenged and loved her. Her money worries were resolved thanks to Grandpa Harrison's contribution, her mother and grandmother were thrilled to bits with their new family addition and they mollycoddled him whenever they got the chance.

Luckily Sebastian adored them right back and treasured having a family who loved and cared for him. They were here together, doing their dream jobs with their two best friends, who Taylor suspected might be announcing a development of their own before too long. She saw the way Selina looked at Patrick, and he followed her around like a lovesick teen half the time. He didn't even notice the adoring nurses anymore. He was pretty much a goner for her old roommate. It was fun watching them skirt and flirt around each other. Perhaps they would have a chapel visit of their own in the not-too-distant future.

She risked a glance back, and he was right behind her. *Almost as fun as sparring with my husband*, she thought, rounding the corner to the skills lab with seconds to spare.

"I win!" she shouted, punching the air with a squeal of triumph. "In your face, Brown!"

Banding his arms around her, he chuckled as he nuzzled her neck. "Wifey, I think we know who the real winner is here."

When she looked up at the adoration etched across his beautiful features, she knew exactly what he was talking about. They had won. They'd overcome their work spats, their differences in life, their families and the struggles it represented to both of them. His father was not part of their lives, and he no longer loomed over them like some specter hiding in the dark. They'd found each other, fought each other, and now they got to live the rest of their lives, doing what they loved and cheering the other on from the front row. No matter where their careers took them, no matter how hard things got or what they faced, they had each other. Had their friends and her family, who would back them no matter what.

Giving up control that night in Vegas, she feared that all of her hard work would be for nothing. Instead, it had been the start of something far more beautiful. Life was messy and chaotic. It could be taken from them in the blink of an eye, altered forever, but they had each other. They had today, and the promise of tomorrow.

"Where did you go?" he asked her softly, knowing that she was in her head again and probably guessing exactly what she was thinking. "Thinking about all the clean clothes you're going to have for a change?"

"No." She smiled, pulling him closer. "I was just thinking that maybe we're both winners here."

His returning grin was dazzling. "I know, baby." Backing her up to the skills lab door, he kissed her again where no one could see them. "I'm the luckiest man in Vegas, and it's all thanks to tequila and Elvis."

* * * * *

If you enjoyed this story, check out these other great reads from Rachel Dove

Hating Dr. Sunshine
One Night to Twin Surprise
Faking It with the Firefighter
A Baby to Change Their Lives

All available now!